WAIT FOR ME

Swoon Series

J.H. CROIX

To mistakes. May they continue to send us in unexpected directions.

Sign up for my newsletter for information on new releases & get a FREE copy of one of my books!

http://jhcroixauthor.com/subscribe/

Follow me!
jhcroix@jhcroix.com
https://amazon.com/author/jhcroix
https://www.bookbub.com/authors/j-h-croix
https://www.facebook.com/jhcroix
https://www.instagram.com/jhcroix/

WAIT FOR ME

He makes an offer I can't refuse. I never thought I was saving myself for anyone. Until Lucas.

Lucas

My priorities are my daughter and my job as a first responder. Romance isn't even on the radar. Until one little package changes everything.

In a single mind-blowing hour, I end up with a package meant for Valentina Smith, and I find out she's a virgin. I won't even mention what's in that package.

Next thing I know, my *other* brain gets the best of me. Valentina deserves the best, so *that* brain says, running my mouth like it has no business.

I don't expect to fall for her. So hard it brings me to my knees. Did I mention she's meant to be worshipped?

Valentina

O.M.G. Hotter than sin Lucas Cole got my package. And opened it. I just knew god had it in for me.

I've got a problem to solve with just the solution. Until Lucas ends up with my, ahem, toy.

Lucas is everything I can't have—hot, broody, and the kind of guy who rescues people for a living. I don't need to be rescued, but I wouldn't mind a taste of the rest.

Chapter One

VALENTINA

Rounding the corner in the hallway, I ran smack into a wall. A wall that turned out to be a person. With two boxes cradled in my arms and a pile of mail on top of that, everything tumbled to the floor. Flustered, I looked straight up into the dark green gaze of Lucas Cole. If he even noticed I'd just dumped mail all over the floor, he didn't show it.

But that was nothing unusual. Neither was the fact my pulse lunged and my body got hot all over. Lucas had that effect on me, and probably most women. He took that whole tall, dark, and broody thing to heart.

"I'm sorry!" I blurted out. "Let me just get all this ..."

My words trailed off because the bad luck of literally running into him only amped up my flustered state and left me breathless. I leaned over to scoop up the mail and bumped my head into his forearm. Dear God. Since when were forearms that hard?

"No worries," Lucas replied as he handed me the mail he had already gathered.

My fingers brushed his as I took it, causing a zing of electricity to race up my arm. Before I could formulate a response, he leaned over and picked up the two small packages. As he handed them over, my brain fired off a thought.

"Oh, one of these is yours," I said, my words coming out rushed.

Juggling the mail and the boxes, I gave him one box. Lucas took it, hooking it in the bend of his elbow. "Thanks. See you around."

With a brief nod, he continued down the hallway. I remained frozen, waiting until I heard his footsteps recede. At the sound of the door closing behind him, I sagged against the wall. Of all the people to run into, it had to be Lucas.

Lucas worked at Stolen Hearts Lodge like me. He was also the sexiest man I'd ever laid eyes on. I could hardly be near him without my body going haywire, as evidenced by this brief encounter. I knew without a doubt that Lucas was *waaaaay* out of my league.

After several deep breaths, I carried on, dropping off the mail in the office and heading to my cabin.

Climbing the steps, I turned to look behind me. The setting sun cast the mountains in shadow. I didn't linger long, not with the small box in my hands. I'd gotten so frazzled seeing Lucas that I forgot about my own mail until I was almost here.

I let myself into my small cabin. This was the first place I'd lived away from my family, so it was ridiculously awesome for me. With only one bedroom, one bathroom, and a pretty view of the Blue Ridge Mountains, it was tiny, but I loved it. Like *loved* it, loved it.

I set the small square box on my dresser. As I held the thin blade of my pocketknife over it, my eyes landed on the label. My heartbeat lunged, and my belly spun in a nervous flip. I was expecting a package, but this was *not* it. For those of us who worked at Stolen Hearts Lodge, all mail came addressed to the lodge, so it was important to pay attention to the return address. Much too late, I noticed this box had the name of a construction supply company on the return address label.

There was only one other person who had received a package in the mail today. Lucas. I'd handed him the wrong one.

"Oh, shit!"

I clapped my hand over my mouth. I didn't know if I'd ever get over that habit. Despite my parents' best efforts, my mouth had a mind of its own. The issue of having the wrong box was worthy of more than one *oh shit*, though.

"Fuck, fuck, fuck."

If only I could apply that word to something beyond a curse. My complete *lack of* in that area was part of my problem right now. I just gave Lucas Cole a box with ...

There was a sharp knock on my door. Startled, I dropped the pocketknife, jumping at the sound of it clattering to the floor. As I leaned over to pick it up, my elbow collided with the corner of the Bible my mother had mailed to me the other day. Like I needed a Bible. The plump book thudded to the floor just as another knock sounded.

My heart was pounding wildly, and I was already about to melt from embarrassment even though I didn't know who was at the door. Not for sure. Ignoring the small mess I'd made on the floor, I squared my shoulders and turned and strode to the door, curling my hand around the knob.

No need to freak out. It's probably not him. On the heels of a deep breath, I opened it and found myself staring into Lucas's green gaze for the second time in an hour.

Shit, fuck, hell, damn.

That was technically only three swear words, and all of them stayed in my brain. You know, like a silent vowel except the entire word was silent. Hell was a place, so it didn't count as a swear. Or so I'd convinced myself at some point during my childhood.

Lucas stood there with an opened box in his hands.

Oh. My. God.

He'd opened the box.

I had the worst luck. Or maybe it was the most embarrassing luck. Was it too much to ask that I have a little dignity around the one man who tended to leave me feeling all swoony and ridiculous?

My eyes, because they were naughty and ignored my mind, meandered over Lucas, taking in his bold features—a strong nose, angled cheekbones, a square jaw with a dark trimmed beard, and sensual lips. Okay, his face was too much. Throw in his to-die-for body—all rangy muscle—and well, I thought God had been a bit too generous in the looks department with Lucas. Just sayin'.

Lucas stared at me quietly, his gaze scanning my face. My cheeks heated the moment I saw his lips quirk with a hint of a smile.

"I think this belongs to you," he said, his voice like sweet sorghum, sliding over me with its slow drawl.

My face was on fire. Hell, it wasn't just my face. *I* was on fire.

"Um, are you sure?" I hedged.

"The address was for the lodge, but it has your name on the receipt in the box," he replied smoothly, losing the battle against his smile.

Not fair! The first time I got to see Lucas smile and it was all because I was an idiot.

"Oh," I replied brilliantly.

He held the box forward, and my eyes—still disobeying me—dropped to look in the box at the hot pink vibrator. It wasn't even hidden. Encased in clear hard plastic, I wouldn't have been surprised if it jumped out of the box and said hello to me, so bold was its presence.

I swallowed and looked back up at Lucas. I couldn't think, much less speak. I now understood how clichés came to be. I was quite certain I might *actually* die of embarrassment. I was hot all over, my pulse had taken off like a rocket

—not joking, it could've propelled me into space—and I felt lightheaded.

Lucas's voice came to me from a distance. "Valentina? Are you okay?"

Nope. Definitely not okay. Everything blurred, and my legs felt wobbly. Then, I fell over.

I seriously fainted in front of Lucas hot-as-sin Cole while he held a box with the vibrator I ordered in his hands.

Chapter Two

LUCAS

Valentina Smith stared at me, her blue eyes wide, and her cheeks nearly as pink as the vibrator in the box. I was doing my damnedest to keep my response to her in check, but you have *no* idea how hard that was. Well, some things *were* most definitely hard. Valentina should've come with a warning sign.

She had curly red hair that practically begged for a man to tangle his hands in it, round blue eyes, and cheeks with freckles dusted over them like gold glitter. She was on the short side and had nothing but curves. She was sex and sin with this hint of innocence to her that made me fucking crazy.

To deal with my out-of-control response to her, I generally ignored her. However, when I tore open this little box and discovered what was inside, holy fucking hell, I had no choice but to come return the package to her. Any other alternative involved someone else, and I could only imagine the less people involved, the better.

It was as if I could hear the beat of time ticking as we faced each other. I gathered she was a bit embarrassed about the situation. Hence, my reason for delivering this personally. Or so I told myself.

My eyes dropped down to the box, and I bit back a chuckle. When I opened the box and saw that vibrator staring back at me, my mouth fell open. I'd been expecting a box with new work gloves. Far more boring than this. I didn't doubt any woman would find satisfaction from this thing. It appeared to have quite a few bells and whistles.

When I looked back at Valentina, her eyes were hazy. I could see the wild flutter of her pulse in her neck and realized she might be about to faint.

"Valentina? Are you okay?"

As I reached over to steady her, she wobbled slightly before collapsing. Fortunately, I caught her by the arm, letting the box fall to the floor as I wrapped my arm around her waist. She was completely out.

I lifted her limp body into my arms and carried her over to the bed, the only obvious option at the moment. There wasn't even a couch in here. It was either the bed or the floor.

Although alarm bells were blaring in my mind—because me, Valentina, and a bed weren't a great plan—I eased her down gently. I quickly checked her pulse to find it was shallow but steady.

I adjusted the pillows under her head and rested my hips on the edge of the bed. Part of me wanted to simply leave at this point. Not because I wanted to leave Valentina after she fainted, but rather, to escape this crazy sense of protectiveness she elicited from me.

With that tangling up in my body's always instantaneous response to her, I needed to be careful. Very careful.

I lifted a hand and brushed a few of her wild red curls away from her forehead, resting the back of my hand against it briefly. Her skin was cool and clammy under the flushed surface.

As a first responder, my instincts to check on things like

that were automatic. Her breaths came in shallow pants, and after a few moments, her eyes opened slowly.

"Well, there you are," I commented, unable to keep from smiling.

Whether it was in relief or this strange sense of joy I experienced being near her, I didn't know. That odd feeling of joy didn't make a lick of sense. Not right now. She had just fainted, for God's sake. I knew she was fine, but still. Her eyes focused on me, slightly confused.

"What happened?"

"You fainted."

She rose on her elbows, her skin turning pink again. "I fainted?"

"Most definitely."

"Did I fall?" she asked as she pushed herself back up on the pillows, looking around.

My eyes lingered on the smatter of haphazard freckles on her cheeks and dropped to the tempting dimple in the center of her plump bottom lip. As she sat up, her T-shirt stretched tight across her generous breasts. I couldn't help but notice the press of her nipples through her bra and the thin cotton shirt.

Dude. What the hell are you doing? She just fainted in front of you, and you're staring at her breasts.

I can't help it. They're near perfect.

That was how bad I had it. My internal debate had a point. I didn't like to think about it, but I had wondered more than once just how her curves felt.

"Lucas?"

Valentina's voice, a soft Southern twang and a little raspy —yes, even her voice dripped sex—punctured my train of thought.

"You didn't fall," I replied, belatedly answering her question. "I was right there, so I caught you."

Her nose wrinkled, and she lifted a hand, nervously twirling one of her curly locks around her fingers. "Oh," she said softly. She caught her bottom lip in her teeth, and I thought I just might not be able to manage myself around her.

I'd never been alone with her. That wasn't unusual. I was rarely alone with any woman. I had a six-year-old daughter who I was raising on my own, which didn't leave much time for anything. I had one priority, and that was Rylie, my little girl.

Usually, I wasn't even tempted. I was busy, fucking busy as hell. Between working as a first responder and working at the lodge and trying to be a parent, sometimes I wondered if I should schedule time to breathe. I didn't know what the hell I would do if my mom and sister weren't around to help me out with Rylie whenever I needed it.

To get to my point, I wasn't easily distracted. But Valentina, damn, the woman distracted me just by existing.

She eyed me warily, her cheeks still pink. "Well, thank you," she said politely. "I guess you saved me."

A grin twitched at the corners of my mouth again. In the past half an hour, with the exception of the time I spent with Rylie, I had smiled more than I had in years.

That was fucking depressing.

"I didn't really save you," I said. "I mean, you would've fallen and maybe sustained a bruise or two. But you'd have been fine. Always glad to help, though."

The temptation to lean forward and kiss her was so insanely strong that I had to force myself to stand abruptly. "Now that you're doing all right, I'll leave you be," I said, stepping back.

Valentina moved swiftly, swinging her legs off the bed and following me over to the door. It was then I realized I had dropped her package in the act of catching her. The vibrator had fallen out and lay on the floor in its molded plastic.

I might've sold my soul to see just what Valentina would be doing with it.

Incongruously, an open pocketknife and a Bible were on the floor as well. I gave my head a quick shake, uncertain what to think of the combination of a vibrator, a Bible, and a pocketknife. I couldn't quite sort out what Valentina had been doing before I arrived unless she had a habit of throwing random items on the floor.

She hurried past me, ignoring the Bible and knife, but picking up the vibrator and flinging it behind her onto the bed. As if we would somehow both forget it had ever been there.

The door to her cabin was still open, and I started to step through it. Just then, her hand caught my wrist. "Lucas," she said, her tone agitated.

With nothing more than the curl of her hand around my wrist, her touch felt like a ring of fire on my skin.

Turning back, I found her standing there, chewing on the bottom lip I wanted to kiss with her cheeks almost as red as her hair. "Yes?"

"Please don't mention this to anyone," she blurted out.

I shook my head. "Of course not. If your name had been on it, I wouldn't have opened it. Just so you know."

She nodded, her hand still around my wrist. "Right. It's just, I know how things get around. Wade's mother is friends with mine, and I might be twenty-five, but my parents still think I shouldn't even kiss a man unless I'm marrying him. I know that's weird, but I love them and ..." She paused to gulp in a breath.

It was downright crazy she thought I would mention this to anyone. I might keep to myself, but I wasn't an asshole. Not to mention, even if I told Wade, he would get a kick out of it, but he sure as hell would *not* tell his mother. As these thoughts passed through, Valentina kept on talking.

"You see, I don't have a boyfriend. I've never had a boyfriend. I wasn't allowed to have a boyfriend. And lately, well ..." She paused here to let out a ragged sigh. "I just thought I should do something about that. I mean it's embarrassing to be a virgin at my age, don't you think? It's just crazy." This time, her pause was nearly electric. "I'd appreciate it if you didn't tell anyone."

Valentina's light touch on my skin left my control hanging by a thread. She was so damn honest it almost hurt, and there were not very many people like that in the world. I couldn't say I knew her well because she'd only started this job at the lodge a few months ago. Wade had mentioned in passing that she'd led a sheltered life and we should all be nice to her, or his mother would give him hell.

I wondered if he had any idea just *how* sheltered her life had been. So there was that, and the fact my brain was about to fucking explode with the knowledge that Valentina was a virgin. That made no sense.

I could *not* fucking believe she had gone through life without some man realizing just how amazing she was. She was beyond beautiful, beyond sexy, and so damn nice. No wonder my body went insane around her.

Now? My mind had jumped on the bandwagon of insanity. Because I couldn't imagine any other man would appreciate her the way I would.

By the time she stopped talking—and I lost track once the word virgin trotted across her lips—I was just staring at her. I took in the elegant arch of her brows, the way her eyes tilted slightly at the corners, the soft curve of her cheek, that sweet dimple in her bottom lip, and her freckles. I'd never considered freckles a temptation, but on Valentina, they were unholy.

I didn't know what she saw cross my face, but she took a deep breath and let it out with a sigh. "Well, I guess maybe I'm asking too much. Please, just don't make it a joke."

I shook my head sharply, both in response to her question and to clear my fucking thoughts. "Valentina, you didn't have to ask me not to tell anybody. I'm a pretty private guy, and I respect your privacy. That's why I brought the box straight to you even though I knew it might be a bit awkward for you to get it from me."

Her eyes widened, and before I realized what she was about to do, she launched herself at me, flinging her arms around my shoulders. "Oh, thank you! I didn't know you were nice."

My arms wrapped around her reflexively, and I felt her feet kick against my shins. She seemed downright overjoyed. She leaned back to look in my face, and I swear it took more discipline than I thought I had not to kiss her.

I eased her down. Then she started talking. Again. "Before you go thinking I'm wacky, I'm not. It's just my parents are kind of religious, and they took the chastity thing a little too far." She paused abruptly and gave her head a shake. "Anyway. Thank you."

Before I had figured out what I was about to say, or that I even had something to say, words strolled out of my mouth. "You know ..." I began, gesturing to her toy, now glowing bright pink on her cream-colored down quilt on the bed, "that's not technically losing your virginity, right?"

Valentina rested a hand on her hip and narrowed her eyes. "Of course, I know that. I just don't want it to be a *thing*. So I figured this would get the hurt part out of the way."

I could *not* believe this conversation. All of a sudden, I found myself envying a fucking vibrator.

Dude, you need to get a fucking grip, my skeptical voice chimed in.

Damn straight, I needed to get a fucking grip, and that meant getting the hell out of here. *Now*.

There was no graceful way to end this conversation, so I held Valentina's gaze and winked. Then I said the craziest fucking thing ever.

"Well, if you decide you need a man to help you out, let me know."

On the heels of that absolutely insane offer, I turned and

left. I had enough sense to close the door behind me. In seconds, I was striding through the trees.

I heard the door fling open again, and Valentina calling, "Lucas! What do you mean?"

I kept walking, but I turned around to see her standing on the small porch, her red hair framing her face in the setting sun with her hands on her hips. Considering that what I'd just said was downright madness, I didn't offer more and forced my feet to keep moving.

Chapter Three

LUCAS

I rolled my truck to a stop in front of my house. After Rylie's mother died, I sold the place where we lived when Rylie was a baby and bought this place. I didn't need memories stained with the mark Melissa left behind.

Grief is fucked up. I had loved Melissa. We had Rylie, and Rylie owned my heart. Whenever I thought back to that first year after Rylie was born—whether I wanted to or not, I picked it apart in my mind time and again—I recalled how differently we handled it. Rylie didn't sleep well for over a year due to colic, but once she got past that, she was the best little sleeper in the world. Melissa never knew because she died before she could find out.

For that year, we were both tired *all* the damn time. Even if you don't mind it, even if you love it because you love the reasons why, when you're that tired, it wears on you. Don't go thinking Melissa was getting up all night on her own. She wasn't. In fact, it was more often me.

After Melissa died, I tore that year to pieces mentally when I found out she'd been having an affair for most of it.

Her affair actually started sooner, but it was that year that bothered me the most. I honestly didn't care about the rest.

An affair gave her something a lot more exciting than a few hours of sleep each night with a colicky baby and a husband who was run ragged between work and trying to hold his family together. That was me.

A ruptured aneurysm killed Melissa. There I was, trying to raise my little girl while grieving the loss of the woman I loved, when I came across the text messages between her and Seth a week later. I wasn't even looking for anything because I'd trusted her. I'd idly picked up her phone as I tried to decide if I should ever turn the damn thing off.

I didn't even know if I would've gone searching for the texts, but one was right there on the screen. They barely tried to cover their tracks. I couldn't help but second-guess if she ever really loved me.

Some people might've said I had baggage. You try being tangled up in grief over someone you thought had loved you, only to find out they'd been having an affair with one of your friends on the side. Yeah, you might say I had trust issues.

I gave my head a hard shake. Rylie had recently turned six and would be starting first grade come autumn. The house we lived in now was tucked in the trees with a small river nearby and about fifteen minutes away from Stolen Hearts Lodge.

Usually when I drove up, I didn't think about anything other than seeing my little girl. Tonight, Valentina came strolling into my thoughts the moment I kicked Melissa out. I had an insane fucking train of thought, wondering how Valentina was with kids.

I climbed out of my truck, shaking that crazy train loose off the tracks in my mind. I opened the front door quietly because it was close to Rylie's bedtime, and sometimes she fell asleep early.

Our house was a small ranch-style home built to blend into the surroundings. With cedar siding and a low-pitched roof, it faced the south to take advantage of the sun. The main entrance led into an open living room with windows running along the front and the kitchen off to the side. Jade waved from the couch with a smile, brushing her hair back from her face. My sister and I shared the same coloring— almost black hair and green eyes. Rylie was curled up beside her, tucked against Jade's side and clearly asleep.

Slipping my shoes off, I walked over to the couch, sinking down onto the cushion on the other side of Rylie.

"Thought you might want to put her to bed," Jade said softly.

"Always."

Rylie stirred. Her bedtime wasn't for another half hour. She lifted her head slowly, rubbing at her eyes with two small fists. "Hey, Daddy," she said as she blinked up at me.

Just like Jade and me, Rylie had dark hair and green eyes. Except for her round button-nose, she was all Cole in her looks. I wondered how much of that would change as she grew up.

"Hey, sweet pea," I said, brushing her tangled hair away from her forehead. "You ready for bed?" Although I could let her stay up for that half hour, I'd learned it was never smart. Not once she was already sleepy. Right now, she'd fall back to sleep fast, but if she stayed up, she'd get her second wind, and bedtime would become a nightmare.

For just a second, I thought she might put up a fight. But she didn't. She nodded. "If you carry me."

I knew there would come a day when she wouldn't want to be carried at all, and frankly, there were plenty of times even now, so I took what I could get. I tugged her onto my lap for a minute, holding her close and pressing a kiss against her hair on the top of her head. "Of course. How'd today go with JJ?"

Ever since she could talk, Rylie had called Jade "JJ," and the nickname just stuck.

"Good. We went for a play date at the park, and then

Grammy came over, and we baked cookies, and she made lunches for you for all week," Rylie explained, her voice sleepy.

"Did she now? I bet you were a big help," I said as I stood with her in my arms.

Jade stood with us and leaned over to press a kiss to Rylie's cheek. "Good night, little one. I'll see you tomorrow, okay?"

"Night, night." Rylie blew Jade a kiss as I turned, adjusting her in my arms.

I walked down the short hallway. There were three bedrooms—Rylie's, mine, and another that was a playroom for her.

Jade, because she was that amazing, had already made sure Rylie changed into her pajamas. Even though I knew the answer, I still asked, "You brush your teeth?"

Rylie's chin bobbed against my chest as she nodded.

"Wash your hands?"

Another nod, this one a little more emphatic.

"Then you're ready for bed."

I eased her down onto her bed, throwing the covers back with one arm as I did. Rylie wiggled into the covers as I tucked them over her. Some nights I read to her, but I could tell tonight was not a book night. Her eyes were already drooping closed as I leaned forward to give her one more kiss. "Good night, sweet pea."

"Night, Daddy," she mumbled.

Sometimes I wondered if my heart would ever stop squeezing when she called me daddy. By the time I reached the door to flick the light off, Rylie's breathing had settled into the steady, even rhythm of sleep. Her butterfly night-light cast a soft glow in the room.

I left the door open a crack and returned to the front of the house. Jade was rinsing dishes and putting them in the dishwasher. "You know you don't have to do that," I said, leaning my elbows on the counter.

Jade closed the dishwasher and turned to face me as she rolled her eyes. "Lucas, you know me. I'm not gonna twiddle my thumbs. I like taking care of stuff. That took me maybe two minutes, tops."

"I know. But you do so much for me," I said as I ran a hand through my hair.

"And you pay me for it. Quite well," she said. "Not that that's entirely necessary, I might add."

"Jade, you gave up a full-time job to help me with Rylie. Of course, I'm gonna pay you. If it weren't for you and Mom, I don't know what I'd do."

"I wouldn't have it any other way. I love that little girl. Don't start with this now, you hear me?" Jade's eyes narrowed.

"Fine, fine. Thank you," I said for probably the thousandth time. Years of her helping me out gave me many chances to thank her.

"Mom will be here tomorrow, okay?"

"I know. Thanks, sis."

Jade picked up her purse off the counter and leaned up to press a kiss to my cheek, squeezing my shoulder as she passed by.

She stopped when she reached the front door. "What?" I asked as she looked at me, her gaze considering.

"Do me a favor," she said.

"Anything," I replied without hesitation.

The moment I saw the gleam in her eyes, I knew I had walked right into that one.

"Stop planning to spend the rest your life alone. You're a good man. You should give some woman a shot."

"Oh, for fuck's sake, Jade. I don't have time for romance."

"I'm not asking you to find time. I'm asking you to be open to the possibility. I'm not deaf, you know. We live in a small town, and people talk. I know you get your needs met, and you manage to find time for that. I guess what I'm saying is I hate seeing you alone. You're one of the best men I know. I know what Melissa did sucked, but it doesn't mean you should block out other options."

She didn't even give me a chance to reply. With a wink and a warm smile, my sister spun away and left, closing the door quietly behind her.

The moment she left, Valentina entered my mind. But I barely knew Valentina. Shaking my head, I forced those thoughts away.

I had one priority. Rylie.

Chapter Four

VALENTINA

The day of the vibrator incident became known in my mind as *Lucas-might-want-me Day*.

After spending days mulling over our surreal encounter, I was still pretty mortified. I wasn't particularly a prude, but I did have some sense of privacy. Not only was it bad enough that he knew I had ordered a sex toy for myself, but then I also had to blabber on about why. I had a big mouth when I was nervous. It was like verbal diarrhea.

I didn't see him again, but that wasn't unusual because working at the lodge kept me busy. Even though I loved my primary job as the accountant and bookkeeper, I also covered shifts at the restaurant when needed. Once a working farm, Stolen Hearts Lodge had morphed into a high-end adventure resort where guests could trek out on various outdoor adventures in the Blue Ridge Mountains while staying here. The lodge also ran a rescue program for animals in the old portion of the farm with a veterinary clinic on site.

Although I had a sheltered childhood, my parents

encouraged me to get a college education. We lived close to one of the state colleges, so I was able to live at home while I attended. My love for numbers led to a degree in accounting, and then I was fortunate enough to have Wade Ellis's mother hook me up with this job. I sensed she was worried about me living at home after graduation. I'd been worried about it too.

I loved my parents, but sometimes they drove me nuts. They were hardcore into Jesus. I believed in God, but I just didn't think God wanted life to be boring. My mother had been wild when she was a teenager, and somewhere along the way, she met my birth father. Everything I knew about him was that he was a rather bumbling and sweet guy. He also liked to party. Hard.

He died in a car accident when he was drunk while my mom was pregnant with me. There my mother was, pregnant with no college degree and no real way to support herself as a single mother.

She made up for her youthful indiscretions by becoming a polite, kind-hearted pastor's wife. The pastor in question adopted me when I was only one year old. I loved my parents dearly even if I chafed against their worries. My mother had been determined not to let history repeat itself.

I wasn't even allowed to date in high school. In fact, I was quite certain if my mother could have her way, I would get married and have a family somehow without ever having sex. My mother even hoped I'd read the freaking Bible she sent me in my spare time. Not that there was anything wrong with the Bible, but I'd already read it cover to cover several times in Bible study.

After the poor Bible ended up on the floor beside my vibrator that fateful afternoon with Lucas, I'd made sure to tuck it away in the bottom drawer of my dresser, safe from accidentally inappropriate moments. Sigh. My life was sometimes ridiculous.

I might be naïve when it came to things like men and sex. However, I was anything but naïve in other ways. With a funny mix of devout and free love in their approach to religion, my parents were about the least judgmental people I knew. They had a variety of people coming in and out of the house—the homeless, criminals, addicts, and more. Once I got older and understood life a bit better, sometimes I wanted to laugh.

They gave everyone a chance even after they'd been burned. My little sister Faith and I had grown up quite savvy. Case in point, we accidentally learned how to cut pills for drug dealing from one visitor to our home. Not that I ever planned to deal drugs.

After college, I started to feel stuck because I had no interest in marrying a pastor or anything like that. I wanted to move on with life.

When Wade's mother pulled me aside after Sunday school one weekend—yes, I helped run the Sunday school daycare because it made my parents happy—and suggested that I take a job here at Stolen Hearts Lodge, I almost squealed right there in the vestibule of the church.

I had my first job outside my parents' church and my own place to live. Being over an hour away from where my parents were was heaven. Although not the kind of heaven I imagined my parents hoped for.

Aside from getting over my guilt for swearing, and that did seem to be sliding off my shoulders, the heaviest baggage I carried related to my complete lack of experience with men. It was beyond ridiculous.

Hence, my decision to buy that crazy hot pink vibrator. I hadn't even used it yet! I was in a bit of a funk. I wished I'd had a boyfriend, or girlfriend, or something in high school. Specifically, someone who wouldn't have expected me to have experience. I wished I'd had something other than the two kisses in my lifetime, both of them sadly disappointing. The worst of the two was from the son of a pastor a few towns over. Not only was he terrible at kissing, but he also pawed at me.

Just thinking about it now caused a little shiver to run through me, and not the good kind of shiver.

Obviously, I'd never kissed Lucas. Yet somehow, I knew beyond a doubt he was good at it. I recalled the flare of heat I saw in his eyes and how my skin prickled with awareness. He was nowhere near me, yet his presence was so potent the mere memory of it managed to send my pulse skittering.

"Hey, Valentina!" Dani Love called from the kitchen.

With a start, I realized I'd been wiping the same table for several minutes. Looking over my shoulder, I saw Dani standing in the doorway at the back of the restaurant. She gave me a little wave.

"Be right there," I called in return as I hurried to straighten the salt and pepper shakers and folded a new set of cloth napkins for the table. By the time I turned back, Dani was out of sight, and the only evidence she'd even been there was the swinging door.

The lodge restaurant occupied roughly half of the ground level of an old barn at Stolen Hearts. Needless to say, it had been renovated to within an inch of its life. Wide plank hardwood flooring ran the length of the restaurant with the windows offering a view of Stolen Hearts Valley. The sun was still high in the sky this afternoon.

Smack in the middle of August, it was so hot I could see the heat shimmering in the air outside. It was air-conditioned in here, and I actually sent up a true prayer of thanks to God for it.

I couldn't even contemplate what summers had been like before air conditioning. If you've never been to the South in the summer, you have no idea how damn hot it can get. It's fry-an-egg-on-the-pavement hot.

Twenty full-time staff worked here, and the ranch could house up to forty guests total, so we stayed busy. After spending most of my life yearning to get out of the Blue

Ridge Mountains, I found it only took being an hour away from my hometown to relax. I'd learned it wasn't the Blue Ridge Mountains specifically that I wanted to escape, but rather the tidy, circumscribed life created by my parents.

Weaving my way around the tables, I headed to see what Dani wanted. With glossy wide plank flooring and square wooden tables, I supposed this décor was considered country chic. I didn't know what else to call it. There was a bar running along the back, and I didn't mind helping myself to it at the end of a long day.

The usual cacophony of noise came at me. The line cooks joked around as they rapidly assembled orders, and another waitress hurried by me with a tray. I gave a wave to the cooks before pushing through another door into the other part of the kitchen. I tended to think of this space as Dani's domain. She was the chef and managed the restaurant.

"Hey, Dani, did you need something?" I asked as I approached her.

She was standing in front of a stainless steel table, staring down at a ball of dough. She glanced up, brushing a stray brown curl away from her forehead with the back of her wrist. "Oh yes, I was hoping you could help me inventory this order we just got in."

"Of course," I replied as I paused beside her. "I don't imagine the order is that ball of dough."

Dani's green eyes brightened with her smile. "Uh, no. The yeast is off in this batch. I thought maybe if I stared hard enough, it would magically rise." With a shrug, she rolled the dough to the end of the table.

Dusting her floured hands on her apron, she nudged her chin to the side. "Come on back here."

Dani was short, like me, and curvy. Her hips swayed as she walked swiftly across the kitchen to a stack of boxes outside the pantry.

"I can take care of this if you need me to. I've gotten pretty used to the system with this," I offered.

"I know you can, but I need something to distract me. I've been making bread all day, and I could use a change of pace."

Just then, Evie Blair came in from the outside, most likely arriving for the dinner shift. She had her straight dark hair pulled back into a ponytail that swung back and forth as she hurried toward us.

"Hey," she said, pausing beside us. "It's hot as hell outside. You been out since this morning?"

Dani shook her head with a grin. "Hell no. It's fucking hot out there. I am a slave to the A/C in the summer."

Meeting Evie's blue gaze, I nodded in agreement. "I'm on Team A/C too."

"Want to get started helping us inventory this order?" Dani asked.

"Sure thing," Evie replied as she hung her purse on a row of hooks by the pantry.

The three of us surveyed the boxes and quickly divided them up. Once we got going, I mostly listened as they chatted. I felt like I hit the jackpot with my first real job—decent pay, a place to live away from home, and really nice people to work with.

Evie rolled her eyes at some comment Dani made about Wade. I might not be an expert in romance, but it was clear as day those two had a thing for each other and probably some history. They were always bickering.

Evie caught my eye and winked. "How much you wanna bet someday Dani's going to have to admit she actually likes Wade?"

I slid my gaze sideways to find Dani glaring at Evie. I shrugged. "A hundred bucks?"

Dani jabbed me with her elbow. "Really? You're going to give me crap too?"

Glancing her way, I shrugged again. "I might not have

been here too long, but it's kind of obvious you like each other."

Dani rolled her eyes and huffed. "Change of subject please. Let's bet on something else."

"How about Lucas getting over himself and actually being a nice guy for once?" Evie offered. "He changed my flat tire for me this morning. He hardly said a word, but I took it as a win."

My ears perked up at that. While everyone seemed friendly with Lucas, I thought perhaps I was the only one he was quiet and broody around.

Dani finished emptying a box of canned olives and rested a hand on her hip as she turned to look at Evie. "Now, you give Lucas a break. He's on the quiet side, but he's never an asshole. He's just all business." She paused, looking from me to Evie. "Things have not been easy for him the past few years. He's a single father. Rylie's mother died when she was only a year old. Then he found out after the fact his wife had been having an affair with one of his friends. That man can be as quiet as he wants."

"Oh! That's terrible," I said, staring at Dani. "Really?"

Dani nodded slowly, leaning down to open a box filled with jars of artichokes. "Yup, it's awful, and that's what happened." She straightened, and her shoulders rose and fell with a sigh. "Melissa did a number on him."

"I can't even believe it. I mean, he's totally hot," Evie chimed in.

Dani's gaze swung to Evie again, her eyes narrowing as she slid two jars onto a shelf. "For God's sake, don't you get hot for Lucas. It's enough to deal with you and Dawson."

Evie's eyes widened. "I am *not* interested in Lucas, or Dawson, for that matter. But you would have to truly be blind not to notice Lucas is handsome as all get-out."

Evie glanced at me, and I felt my cheeks heat. Suddenly, they were both looking my way. "What?" I blurted out.

"I dunno," Evie said. "But your cheeks are all red. Do you have a thing for Lucas?"

Dani bit her lip, fighting a smile.

"No. I do not," I lied. "Just like you, I might have noticed he's handsome. That's all. Y'all know my life. When it comes to men, I get embarrassed about anything."

I so, *so* wanted to tell them about the disaster with the vibrator, but I couldn't bring myself to. At that moment, conveniently, one of the line cooks called for Dani just as the hostess called back to let us know we had a new table to cover. Evie volunteered to take it, seeing as my shift was almost over.

Dani hurried off to take a call, leaving me alone to finish doing the inventory and unpacking the supplies. All the while, I couldn't forget Lucas's last comment.

"Well, if you decide you need a man to help you in these matters, let me know."

I wondered just what he meant by it, and whether I could scramble up the nerve to ask.

———

Kicking the sheets loose from my feet, I rolled over in bed with a sigh. I was chasing sleep to no avail. When I opened my eyes, a sliver of moonlight falling at an angle through the window beside my bed illuminated the room. The sheets were damp and stuck to my skin. Shimmying my hips, I loosened the cotton twisted around my waist and lifted it, letting the air gust across my body as the sheet drifted back down.

My nipples were tight, and the sensation of the thin cotton on my skin abraded them. My mind spun to Lucas.

He was the reason I was hot and sweaty and grasping for sleep that wouldn't come. To be fair, it was *me* obsessing over him that was at fault. A sigh slipped from my lips, and my belly clenched at the memory of his intense gaze on me. I shifted my legs restlessly. Before I thought about it, I was reaching between my thighs and teasing into the slick heat there.

I might not be able to have Lucas, but that didn't stop me from fantasizing about him. My climax came quickly, and blessedly, sleep finally claimed me in the aftermath.

Chapter Five

LUCAS

I stood in the shower, leaning my hands against the tile and savoring the feel of the hot water beating down over me. Considering I'd been covered in sweat and dirt when I walked in here and hot as could be, I couldn't believe how much I was enjoying the hot shower. I started it out cold, though, to knock the sticky heat off.

Today had been insanely busy. Just the way I liked it. It had started out with a call to an accident on a narrow mountain road. After that, I spun into the lodge and picked up a guided hike. I led a group of college kids on an eight-mile hike up and down the mountain today. One woman spent half the time flirting with me, and even though she was beautiful, I couldn't have cared less.

I'd barely spared much more than a passing thought about women ever since Melissa died. She'd soured me on the idea of love. Being a single father, I found I didn't have much time for women, and when I did, I kept it casual. As the steaming water beat down on my sore muscles, Valentina danced through my thoughts.

Valentina should have given me pause. She screamed

innocent in some ways, yet in others, she seemed too wise for her years. Her innocence drew me in, and it shouldn't. Hell no.

Try as I might, I could *not* forget what happened last week. Not for a second. As usual, I'd been so damn busy I could hardly keep my head up. But she'd been occupying a corner room in my thoughts so thoroughly it was like she had moved into my brain.

Virgin. Valentina was a fucking virgin. Somehow, I could *not* stop thinking about that. Or how she ran her mouth about how she ended up with that vibrator. I couldn't help but wonder if she'd taken it for a test run.

Just thinking about *that* caused my cock to swell. Fuck. Pushing away from the wall, I swiftly turned the knob to cold water. Problem solved. I was in the shared showers for the guys at the lodge. Although I didn't live here as some staff did, all of us were allowed to use any of the facilities.

I intended to grab a bite of dinner here before heading out. I preferred to shower here before I went home, if only because the minute I walked through the door, Rylie would latch on to my side.

I quickly toweled dry and dressed in clean jeans and a T-shirt. Grabbing my bag, I strolled down the hallway toward the staff kitchen. When I entered, Dani was busy at the stove. Meanwhile, Jackson, Shay, Dawson, Walker, and Grace were sitting at the massive table in the back of the kitchen.

Dropping my bag on the floor by the door, I paused by Dani's side. "Need me to carry anything over?"

She glanced up with a smile as she turned a burner off. "No, thank you. You go sit down. Food's already on the table." I started to turn, but her voice pulled me back. "Actually, on second thought, grab some beer and wine. I know you won't drink any since you're driving home, but the rest of us will."

Striding to the industrial-size stainless steel refrigerator, I snagged a six-pack of beer and grabbed a bottle of wine as

I passed by the rack. As I approached the table, I glanced up, my eyes immediately landing on Valentina's dark red curls. She must've come in through the back.

It felt as if a bolt of lightning struck my body. Fuck me. I shouldn't want her the way I did, but there was no denying how badly I wanted her. My entire body tightened in anticipation, a hum of electricity zinging through me.

I scanned the large picnic table with enough space for ten or more. I never knew the cluster of staff I would find here. Sometimes it was just a few, and other times it was a full house.

In the few moments since I had entered, the table had filled up. Dani beat me there with another platter, sliding her hips down on the last seat at one end, leaving me with only one choice of where to sit. Right beside Valentina.

Ignoring my body's response to her, I strode to the table, setting the beer and wine in the middle before slipping onto the end of the bench seat. Voices were crossing over each other as everyone talked. Valentina replied to something Grace said and laughed at a joke from Dawson.

If my state around her wasn't ridiculous enough already, a flash of possessiveness surged inside. Dawson was a good guy and a friend, but he was a consummate flirt. Him teasing Valentina was par for the course, as it was with every woman he had a chance to tease.

Case in point, Dawson glanced over at Shay, the new love of Jackson's life, and then at his boss and winked shamelessly. "Shay keeping you in line?" Dawson teased.

Jackson simply shook his head and chuckled, his arm resting over Shay's shoulders. I imagine he intended to eat with one hand. That man was whipped. Good thing Shay so clearly adored him.

I reached for the pitcher of water in the center of the table, my arm brushing Valentina's elbow as I did. She glanced my way, her stunning blue eyes colliding with mine.

"Oh! I didn't realize that was you, Lucas," Valentina said, a blush cresting on her cheekbones.

"I just sat down," I replied, stating the obvious, as I was wont to do when I felt off balance.

I didn't get nervous often. In fact, I could probably count on one hand the number of times I'd actively experienced nervousness. Yet Valentina appeared to have the unique ability to set my nerves to sparking.

"Of course you just sat down," she replied, her lips curling into a slight smile.

My eyes snagged on that little dimple in her bottom lip, and my cock twitched. *Cut that shit out*, I mentally ordered.

"How are you?" I asked, looking away to fill my water glass.

"I'm quite fine. How are you?"

Before I had a chance to reply, Dani nudged my hand from across the table with a platter. "Lasagna?" she asked.

Glancing up, I smiled. It was hard *not* to smile at Dani. I'd known her forever, and she was good people. "Is there anything I don't want if you're cooking?" I asked as I took the platter from her and served myself.

Dani chuckled. "I don't think so although you're not a fan of the vegetarian options."

I laughed softly. "I like vegetables fine, just not all by themselves."

Another comment from someone drew Dani's attention away. "I'll take some lasagna," Valentina offered.

"How much?"

Nothing was unusual about me serving whoever happened to be sitting beside me. We all did. It was a casual dinner among friends.

Yet everything felt loaded with Valentina now. Between every sentence, I remembered she was a virgin and how she thought it was something she needed to deal with. I couldn't imagine any other man having *any* part of that, which was crazy thinking on my part.

"How much?" I pressed.

"About half of what you got. Lord knows, you boys eat so much I don't even know how you manage it."

Dawson, of course, just had to chime in. "Darlin', we can manage more than that."

Dani sent him a pointed look. "You be nice to Valentina."

"What did I say that wasn't nice?" Dawson protested.

"You are always teasing, and sometimes it's a bit much."

Dawson rolled his eyes. Meanwhile, after I served Valentina, I passed the platter over to Dawson who was already teasing someone else.

I ate quickly, trying not to notice Valentina's subtle citrusy smell. I wanted to wrap my hand in her red hair and kiss her senseless.

These were thoughts I shouldn't be having. I glanced up at the clock on the wall behind the table as I was mopping up the last of the lasagna on my plate with some garlic bread. "I gotta roll," I said after my last bite.

Standing, I couldn't resist one last look at Valentina. She glanced up. "Good night, Lucas," she said.

Of course, my eyes just *had* to dip down and notice the hint of her cleavage in the V-neck T-shirt she wore. Sweet Jesus, the last thing I needed to notice was that tease of navy blue lace along the curve of her breast.

Chapter Six

VALENTINA

"Mom, you don't need to worry. I'm doing great," I said into the phone.

"Hon, it sure sounds like you are, but let me worry. You're my first child to move away from home," she replied.

I bit back a sigh. Her point was completely accurate, but the urge to shake free of her worries was fierce sometimes.

"I'll let you worry, Mom. Just do me a favor and try to have faith I'll be fine."

Her laughter rang in my ear. "Oh, you are good! Of course I have faith in you." She paused, her voice muffling to say something to someone else. "Sorry about that. I've gotta go. You call me next week, okay?"

"I always do, Mom. Love you."

Hanging up, I smiled. Much as I'd worried my parents would pressure me more to move back home, they'd gracefully accepted my choice to take this job. If that meant I needed to listen to my mother worry when we talked every week, then I could deal with it.

With a mental shake, I returned my attention to work. Staring at the spreadsheet in front of me, I let my breath out slowly. Numbers calmed me. I loved numbers and spread-sheets, really anything that helped me feel organized.

I settled in to spend the morning reconciling the accounts for last month. Roughly an hour later, a soft knock sounded on my door. Glancing up, I saw Shay Martin smiling at me.

I removed my glasses and set them on the desk. "Hey, how's it going?"

Shay stepped into my office—I still couldn't believe I had my own office sometimes—and slipped into the chair across from my desk. "Good. I was just thinking I am *so* freaking glad Jackson thought it was a good idea to have you help with the accounting. It's only been two months, and I can't even put into words how much less stressed I am now."

From what I understood, Shay had largely taken over the business end of things around here. Stolen Hearts Lodge used to work with an accountant based out of Asheville, but when I had applied for the job here and they learned I had handled the accounting for my parents' church and retreat organization for the past few years, Shay promptly told Jackson they needed me for more than basic bookkeeping and waitressing.

My smile stretched as I looked at Shay. She couldn't know how much it meant for me to have this job. It was just a job, but it was so much more for me.

"Well, I love it, so I'm glad that it helps you out. I don't even know how you do everything you do," I added.

She shrugged lightly. "I like to be busy. Plus, I love the animals."

I'd pieced together since I'd started here that she and Jackson were a fairly new couple. It was plain as day that Jackson was head over heels in love with Shay, and she returned the feeling. I hoped if I ever got a chance like that, I would find a man who loved me as much as Jackson loved her.

"Speaking of things to do, I keep meaning to take you

with me when I feed the animals. That way, you can be my backup if I'm busy. Actually, Jackson and I will be gone for a couple of days next week, so I was hoping you wouldn't mind handling that."

"Of course not. Anything to spoil Gloria and Squeaky is fun for me."

I was referring to a giant pig and a mini pig, respectively. They were two rescue pigs who had become permanent residents at the lodge. With Gloria a few hundred pounds larger than Squeaky, they made a cute pair.

"What time?" I asked as I glanced down and hit save on my spreadsheet.

"Not until this evening. That's the only way for you to get to see everything. Are you on shift tonight at the restaurant?" Shay asked as she reached up and tightened the elastic on her ponytail. She was beautiful with dark blond hair and green eyes. I was slowly getting to know her even though I hadn't had a ton of girlfriends growing up.

My parents' unique combination of being devout and hippie dippy meant they didn't fit in many circles. With me being homeschooled, I didn't have many opportunities to make friends my age.

"Tonight's perfect. I'm not on duty at the restaurant."

"Great. Will you still be here around five?"

"I'll be here all day. I'm reconciling the accounts for last month. I like to do it all in one chunk so I don't lose track," I explained.

She grinned. "Awesome. I'll come get you when it's time. I'm across the hall if you need anything. Jackson has appointments in the vet clinic all day, so you might want to close your door. You know it can get a little noisy with the animals coming in and out."

"You got it. I'm gonna refill my coffee," I said as I stood from my desk.

"Oh good, I need some too. Let's make a fresh pot. Knowing Jackson, he's already drained the last pot."

I followed Shay down the hall. When I had started working here, they reorganized the layout of the offices. My office used to be an old exam room for the vet clinic. It was tiny, but I adored it. In the corner of the renovated upper floor of the barn, it was a perfectly square room with cream painted walls and a window that looked out over the Blue Ridge Mountains. They had also converted a storage space into another exam room and expanded the space in the front of the clinic.

Jackson saw patients or, rather, pets on the days he worked in the clinic. I didn't know how he managed it all. Between being a first responder for Stolen Hearts Valley Emergency Response, running the lodge and rescue program, and managing his part-time veterinary clinic, he was beyond busy.

He had a lot of help, though. Shay worked double duty, handling most of the administrative stuff for the clinic, lodge, and rescue program. Wade and Lucas helped Jackson with the renovations over here. I didn't even know how they fit all that in between everything else, but they completed them within just a few weeks. Shay was now looking to hire a vet tech to help Jackson.

We walked together into the front where we had a counter at the back that held a coffeemaker, a teapot, and a microwave. Jackson's voice carried to us as he walked out with an owner and their pet.

"I think she'll be just fine," he said.

"Are you sure, Jackson?" a female voice asked in return with a most definite flirtatious tone to it.

When Shay caught my eyes, she rolled hers in return. I had noticed that many pet owners enjoyed flirting with Jackson. Shay was a good sport about it, but then it was beyond obvious that Jackson completely adored her.

I started prepping the coffee as Shay waited by the register. When Jackson came into view, he glanced over at Shay and winked. The pet owner in question was a pretty woman with short dark hair and dark eyes to match. She had an athletic, energetic vibe to her and held a tiny Chihuahua in her arms.

Jackson stepped around the back of the counter and leaned over to press a kiss against Shay's cheek. "Ellen doesn't owe us anything. It was just a follow-up from the surgery last week."

"Oh, great. Let me give you the printout so you have it for your records," Shay replied, smiling over at Ellen.

Ellen's eyes bounced back and forth between Shay and Jackson, and I could see a flicker of disappointment in her gaze. Jackson was generally oblivious to the women who flirted with him and likely didn't even kiss Shay to make a point. It was just that whenever he saw Shay, he had to put his hands on her. Of that, I was certain.

Jackson turned around just as I tapped the start button on the coffeemaker, resting his hips against the counter. "There'll be enough for me, right?" he asked with a smile.

"I should hope so," I replied.

Jackson was a handsome man with shaggy brown hair and blue eyes. As I looked at him, I idly wondered how come my body didn't spin like a top around him or, frankly, most of the other men who worked here. Seeing as they were a combination of first responders and adventure guides, they were all fit and rugged, yet Lucas was the only one who got me hot and bothered.

I bit my lip, my cheeks getting warm just thinking about him. With his passing comment that I should let him know if I wanted a *man* to help with those matters, I couldn't stop thinking about whether he really meant it. I didn't need to remember how I'd finally done a test run with my shiny new vibrator with him in mind.

My mind went *right* there. A vivid recollection of Lucas's rich green gaze, the feel of his muscular body against mine when I'd impulsively hugged him—that was all it had taken to send my thoughts strolling into a fantasy the other night.

My fingers teasing my slick folds had been Lucas's in my imagination, and my magic pink vibrator had been him stretching me. My climax rolled through me so rapidly it had taken me by surprise.

When Shay turned back to face us as the owner and her Chihuahua left, just recalling those moments of intense fantasy left me so flustered that I had to busy myself by needlessly wiping the counter around the coffeemaker. After pouring coffees for all of us, Shay tugged me into a conversation with Jackson about the shelter rescue, promptly getting my mind off Lucas.

"I promise, the horses are easy," Jackson assured me. "They might be big, but they're creatures of habit."

"They all seem nice enough when I stop and pet them. It's just I've never fed them. That easy, huh?"

"If you're worried, I can ask ..." Jackson began.

At that moment, the door opened, drawing the attention of all three of us. I expected to see any number of pets coming in with an owner. Instead, Lucas stepped through the door with an absolutely adorable little girl in his arms.

Without question, I knew she was his daughter. And, oh my God, was she ever cute. Her features were softer than his, and her hair was curly to his mostly straight, but she was the spitting image of her father with black hair and bright green eyes. I'd never seen Lucas over here except when he helped with the renovations. Jackson and Shay looked just as surprised as me.

"Hey Lucas," Shay said with a smile. "What brings you over here?" She rounded the counter, heading straight for him and plucking his daughter from his arms. "And you, sweet Rylie, what are you doing here? It's my lucky day."

Shay nuzzled Rylie's cheek as Rylie giggled, putting her small arms around Shay's neck and planting a noisy kiss on her cheek.

Lucas watched them for a beat before answering Shay's question. "I'm in a bit of a bind. I'm on call for the team, and my sister's sick today. My mom is also tied up at a doctor's appointment. I wouldn't ..."

His words tapered off as Shay nodded firmly. "We've got Rylie. You go do what you need to do."

The lines of tension eased on his face. "Well, it's either that, or Jackson covers for me on duty through tonight. I don't want to impose."

Shay glanced at me. "I'm sure Valentina and I can handle Rylie."

"Of course we can," I heard myself saying. "We'll have fun."

Lucas just now seemed to notice me. His eyes widened slightly when they met mine.

Jackson glanced back and forth between us and then back at Lucas. "Normally, I'd cover for you, but today's a clinic day, and I'm booked solid. You know Rylie's in good hands."

Rylie giggled as she spun one of her curls around her finger.

"Come meet my friend, Valentina," Shay said as she turned and walked over to me.

I set my coffee down and leaned forward. "Hi. I don't think we've met. Tell me your name."

"Rylie!" she said as if making an announcement to the universe.

I held out my hand, and Rylie squeezed it in hers. "Nice to meet you. I'm Valentina."

"Valentine," Rylie said with a nod, her curls bouncing.

Lucas had followed Shay over. "You mind being called Valentine?" he asked, his gaze sliding sideways to mine.

I tried to tell my body to behave, but it was having none of that. Heat bloomed from my chest outward, and my belly did a little flip. I was quite certain Lucas wasn't being the least bit flirtatious. It was just that he had that effect on me.

"Not at all," I replied, hoping my voice didn't sound as breathy as it felt.

"Shay's helped out in a pinch before. You had much experience with kids?" he asked.

"More than enough. I used to babysit all the time for my little sister and helped run the daycare at my parents' church for the kids who were too young for Bible study."

"What's Bible study?" Rylie asked as Shay lowered her to the floor.

"It's where people talk about a big book," I explained.

Lucas's low chuckle sent a shiver over my skin. "Excellent description," he countered, his tone deadpan.

"If you got a call, I'm guessing you're in a hurry," Shay chimed in.

"Always," Lucas said, his eyes bouncing to her. "Hang on, let me grab her snacks from the car. I was in such a hurry I didn't even get those on the way in."

"I'll follow you out," I heard myself offering.

Seeing as Rylie was clearly comfortable with Shay, I figured it was best if I helped out on this end. Lucas's long stride ate up the distance from the clinic to his truck while I hurried behind him.

"You sure you don't mind?" he tossed over his shoulder as he stopped beside the vehicle.

"Of course not. I love kids."

His truck was black and sleek. The outside fit his personality. The inside was another matter. In the back seat, the booster seat and just about everything else was pink.

"I'm guessing your daughter likes pink," I offered as Lucas leaned in and curled his hand around the handles of a pink bag.

He turned back, a half grin kicking up one side of his mouth. "She loves pink. Though she's a tomboy, and most of her toys are trucks."

He handed me the bag. "There's a lunch in there and some snacks. I gotta run."

"Of course you do," I replied as I reached for the bag, my

hand brushing his. A hot zing spiraled up my arm from that brief contact.

Lucas held my gaze for a long moment, and my insides went molten.

"Thank you." He paused and pulled out his phone. "Give me your number, so I can text when I'm on my way back."

I recited it quickly, and he tapped it into his phone. In a second, I felt a vibration in my pocket where my phone was.

"Just confirming," he said.

I pulled it out and showed him the text. "That you?"

"Absolutely. Seriously, thanks." At that, he hopped in his truck.

I watched as he drove away.

Chapter Seven

VALENTINA

"So," Shay said as she paused with a hand on her hip, "this is where all the food is. At least for the horses. We keep treats for basically every creature here as well."

We were in the tack room. It was a large, square room with windows high on the wall. Since the barn was built halfway into the hill, on this lower floor, the storage rooms along the back wall had windows at the top. There was a hallway and two rows of stalls on the other side.

"Got it." Rylie had wandered over and was investigating the bins. We had a fun day with her, taking turns keeping her entertained, and then when she got tired this afternoon, she napped in one of the comfy chairs in Shay's office. "I'm guessing I should stock up on treats before anything else?" I asked, glancing at Shay.

"Oh yeah," Shay replied.

"Want to carry some treats?" I asked Rylie.

She nodded vigorously, her black curls bouncing with the motion.

Shay flicked open the lids on some of the bins mounted against the wall. "There's dried fruit for Gloria ..."

"The pig!" Rylie exclaimed.

She laughed softly. "Yes, the big pig. It's dog bones for the dogs, and grain treats for everyone else."

Shay snagged a handful of everything, filling her pockets and putting some in the small pockets of Rylie's lightweight jacket.

All in all, it took about an hour between feeding the horses and crossing the pasture to the other barn where the rest of the rescues stayed. Gloria and Squeaky kept us company. Gloria was a friendly sort and made snuffling noises to Rylie's delight when she fed her a piece of sliced apple. Squeaky was just as affectionate and lived up to her name with squeaks.

After we returned to the clinic, I began to wonder when we would hear from Lucas. Apparently, the team had responded to an accident in a remote area. The winding roads of the Blue Ridge Mountains could be a challenge under good circumstances, and in some areas, they were dicey.

Shay and I were chatting in my office after I had finished reconciling the accounts, enjoying a late cup of coffee while Rylie played with toy horses and shredded paper on the floor. The shredded paper was a great option for hay in her imaginary barn.

"Jackson thinks we can add another barn for additional space for the rescue program. We have the land, but my concern is the time. With you here helping with the accounts ..." Shay stopped talking when the emergency buzzer rang from the main entrance.

Jackson was finishing up with his last appointment, and we had locked up just a few minutes ago.

"I'll go see who it is," Shay said, standing and hurrying down the hallway.

Moments later, she leaned around the door. "We have an emergency, so I'm going to help Jackson. Do you mind staying with Rylie until we hear from Lucas?"

"Of course not," I replied quickly.

With a quick nod, she hurried away. I glanced over at Rylie who was cantering the horse in her hand through the paper hay. I left my coffee on the table and sat down beside her on the floor. "Want to race?" I asked, lifting another one of the toy horses.

Rylie grinned up at me. We settled into a silly game of racing. Roughly a half an hour passed, and Rylie had moved on to playing a card game on her own. I realized I hadn't heard a thing from Shay or Jackson down the hallway. Glancing at the clock, I saw it was about time for her evening snack, which consisted of a half a peanut butter and jelly sandwich and apple slices.

While she ate, I checked to discover Jackson was handling emergency surgery for a dog who'd been hit by a car. Shay was running interference with the distraught mother and child who brought the dog in. I assured Shay I would stay with Rylie until we heard from Lucas.

With darkness falling, it was no surprise when Rylie nodded off into another nap. By the time Lucas texted to say he was on his way back, she was sound asleep. I replied to ask him to text me when he got to the parking lot. It wasn't much later he responded.

I'm here, Valentine.

I didn't know if his text had autocorrected to Valentine, but it made me smile. Rylie was groggy when I woke her, but she followed along easily. I had wisely packed up everything beforehand.

With her hand warm in mine, and the bag hooked over my elbow, I left through the side door at the end of the hallway rather than interrupting the family waiting in the front area. It was dusk, the sky slipping from silvery gray into navy. The light was smudgy with the lavender and pink streaks the sun left behind bleeding into the sky as night claimed it.

Lucas climbed out of his truck when he saw me. When I

looked up across the parking lot, my heart gave a resounding thud, and my pulse took off at an unsteady gallop. When I stopped in front of him, Lucas's eyes went to Rylie first, his lips curling with a slight smile. My pulse kept on running.

He ruffled her hair. "Hey there, let's get you in the truck."

Rylie released my hand as he opened the back door of his four-door truck. He lifted her smoothly when her foot slipped as she climbed in. He deftly buckled her into the booster seat and took her bag from me, tucking it into the front before quietly closing the door. Glancing through the window, I saw her eyes had already fallen closed again.

Only then did he turn, leaning his hip against the truck. His green eyes stood out in the gloaming. "Figured she'd be tired. Thanks again. That took longer than I thought," he said, his voice low. "How was she?"

"She was fine. No problems at all. It was a busy afternoon, so I'm not surprised she's tired. We took her with us to feed the animals."

Lucas's mouth kicked up just barely at one corner, and my belly promptly executed a flip. My mind skidded back to the afternoon last week, and my cheeks got hot while my thoughts went off in a rather inappropriate direction.

"I bet she loved that." Lucas's voice broke into my runaway train of thought.

I mentally snapped the reins on my willful mind. Lucas's gaze slid sideways into the back of his truck. I could barely make out Rylie with her head tilted back as she slept.

I was suddenly envious of her ability to sleep so well. I hadn't been sleeping well. In fact, my nights were restless with tangled, sweaty dreams usually involving Lucas.

Glancing back at him, I found his gaze on me. I didn't quite know how he pulled the trick off. All he had to do was look at me, and my belly felt funny, and a restless feeling stole through me.

It didn't help matters that his presence was so potent. His eyes flicked into the truck windows again.

The lingering humidity in the air only amped up the heat building inside. Lucas turned back, catching me staring at him. His lips curled into a smile again. My body *knew* this smile was nothing like the one he had when I mentioned we took her to feed the animals.

My pulse, which had barely slowed down, took off into the stratosphere, humming along so fast, I could hardly catch my breath. Lucas cocked his head to the side, his gaze considering.

"So tell me, how are you?"

I was relieved for the smudgy light of dusk and hoped like hell he couldn't see just how flushed I was. I shrugged, striving for nonchalance. "Just fine."

He leaned forward slightly, closing the distance between us and peering into my face. "Fine? I'm never sure what fine means."

I narrowed my eyes and glared at him. "It just means I'm fine."

I couldn't say why his simple question felt loaded, nor why I glared at him. My skin felt itchy with pinwheels of sensation pricking it all over.

Some people might say I had led a sheltered life, and I had. Sheltered or not, I was quite certain having a man you kind of had a crush on accidentally get your package with a vibrator in it did not fall under something that happened to many people. I didn't know how to do regular conversation after that.

I stayed quiet. Frankly, I didn't know what to do other than laugh at the ridiculousness of the situation.

What I said next surprised the hell out of me. "I'm sorry about last week," I blurted out.

Lucas straightened, his gaze never breaking from mine. "Sorry for what?"

I shrugged. Gah! None of this made sense. "It was just

kind of, well, embarrassing, and now it's all awkward, and I hate that."

"You don't need to apologize. There's also no need—" He paused and gave his head a shake. "You know, you're so beautiful I can't think straight."

His words shocked the hell out of me, even more so coming at me sideways like that. "No shit?" I couldn't believe he thought I was beautiful.

When I reflexively slapped my hand over my mouth, Lucas graced me with another one of his smiles. This time, my belly did several flips as if in celebration.

"No shit," he said dryly.

In the category of shocking the hell out of me and turning my world upside down, he then reached out to catch one of my hands in his. Before I registered what was happening, he reeled me close to him. I thought he was potent before, but the moment I was standing immediately in front of him, I was almost on fire.

"I've been thinking again ..." He paused as if to gather his thoughts.

Because I was me, and my mouth just wouldn't quit when I was anxious, I jumped in. "About what? Because I've been thinking too. I think it would be a great idea for you to tell me what you meant when you said if I needed any help to let you know. Because I need some help. In fact, I think you're just the man to help me."

His gaze was on me, practically searing. I wasn't sure how to read what I saw there. It might be desire, but I wasn't so sure I could trust my body. It had gone haywire with butterflies spinning in mad circles in my belly, my pulse skittering out of control, and my sex clenching. God, I just wanted to touch him all over. He was downright yummy.

His mouth barely hitched at one corner. "Maybe you ... I'm not saying you should wait for me. I'm just saying ..." His words ran out.

For once in my life, I didn't step in to fill the silence. I felt as if I were leaning over the edge of a cliff waiting for him to finish whatever he was going to say.

"I guess what I meant to say is you deserve the real deal."

My nose itched like it did whenever I got nervous. I lifted a hand, rubbing my nose vigorously with my knuckles. Lucas stayed quiet, but I could sense he was waiting for me.

"I think that's a great idea. When?"

"Damn, darlin', you just get right to the point, don't you?"

"Yes. I don't see any sense in beating around the bush."

"I guess I'll never have to worry about you not making it clear what you mean," he said, almost as if to himself. "Rylie's spending next weekend with her grandparents. I'll be here for the weekend because Jackson will be gone."

Just to be sure, I asked, "So next weekend, then?"

"Maybe. We'll take it one step at a time."

Then he went and shocked the hell out of me all over again.

"Starting right now," he said so softly I leaned forward to hear him.

Conveniently, he was leaning down, his hand sliding into my hair just before he brought his mouth to mine. Like I said, I'd been kissed before. But sweet Jesus, I had *never* been kissed like this.

His lips brushed over mine softly. I sighed at the feel of his fingers lacing into my hair, sending tingles racing down my spine. I thought he said my name, but I couldn't hear over the rush of blood in my ears. When his tongue swiped across the seam of my lips, I pretty much threw myself at him, climbing him like a tree as I wound my arms around his neck.

He made a sound, almost pained, and palmed my bottom with his other hand. I definitely noticed the hard ridge of his arousal against my belly, and it only sent me spinning higher inside. On a gasp, his tongue swept into my mouth, gliding sensually against mine.

I lost track of everything—everything but the feel of Lucas, his strong hold, and his mouth working over mine. Just as I was on the verge of melting, he eased me down, murmuring my name softly as he drew away.

I heard the soft sound of protest coming from my throat and had to bite my tongue to keep from pleading with him not to stop. His eyes met mine in the almost darkness.

"Trust me, I don't want to stop, darlin'. But I have a sleeping girl in the truck, and I need to get her home."

I had been so thrown into the moment I had entirely forgotten about Rylie sound asleep in the back seat of his truck. Whatever he saw on my face must've translated to mortification because he leaned forward and pressed his lips to mine in a quick kiss.

"I'll see you before next weekend. You can count on that."

Chapter Eight

LUCAS

"Well, what do you think?" Dani asked.

I leaned across the table, eyeballing the schedule she was working on. Dani was a total fan of color-coding everything. My color was green. According to Dani, this was because it matched my eyes.

It did, technically speaking. Yet I found it amusing that was how she color-coded. I remained puzzled as to how she managed the colors. Dawson had been given purple, which I guess was a variant of his gray eyes.

Dani cleared her throat, flipping a pencil back and forth between her fingers.

"That'll work," I finally replied.

"So you'll take care of three of the hikes that weekend. That's going to be okay?"

"Sure is. Rylie's grandparents have her for four days, so I'll stay out here to save myself the bother of running home every night," I explained.

Dani pushed one of her brown curls behind her ear and smiled. "Perfect. How is Miss Rylie?"

"She's good. But she's always good," I replied with a

smile. If there was one thing in the world guaranteed to make me smile, it was my daughter.

"And how are you?" Dani asked next.

"Right as rain."

Dani began flipping that pencil back and forth again, cocking her head to the side and casting me a considering gaze. "Are you really, Lucas? As far as I can tell, all you do is work. Well, that and be an amazing father to Rylie."

I'd known Dani for years and considered her a friend. Her only negative qualities were her nosiness and her shameless tendency to be pushy.

"I think that's more than enough," I said with a roll of my eyes as I pushed away from the table in her office and stood.

At that moment, there was a soft knock on the open door. Glancing over my shoulder, I found Valentina standing there. Her glorious dark red hair was pulled up in a ponytail, but that did barely anything to tame it. Her curls went every which way. One had fallen loose to dangle down the side of her cheek. I wanted to reach out and catch it and pull her to me.

The mere sight of her was a shock to my system—a hard, electric jolt—and a tightening followed.

"Oh, am I interrupting?" Valentina asked quickly. "I knocked before I realized you were in here."

"I didn't close the door, and it's impossible for me to care about interruptions," Dani said with a laugh as she waved Valentina into her office.

Valentina's eyes flicked to me. I didn't miss the subtle flush that crested her cheeks. As I looked at her—because I couldn't *not* look at her—I became acutely aware of the dusting of freckles sprinkled across her nose and cheeks and wondered if she had freckles everywhere.

I'd just about convinced myself I lost my fucking mind the other night when I kissed her. Even crazier when I proposed whatever the hell it was I proposed for this weekend. But I couldn't forget it, not the feel of her inviting lips under mine nor the press of her breasts against my chest. It didn't matter if I was crazy. I wanted Valentina, and I would have her.

There was only one problem. She didn't fit into the tidy place I had carved out in my life for women. Ever since Melissa died and I found out who she really was, well, you could say I was bitter. Just a tad.

The concept of trust was hard to come by. So I kept things entirely superficial. I had once been the guy my friends teased for settling down young and being excited to start a family. Oh, I was no saint before that. I sowed my wild oats in high school and college. But when Melissa came along, I fell hard for her.

We hadn't planned to have Rylie as soon as we did, but once Melissa was pregnant, I was all in. After she died and I came to terms with the illusions I'd had about her and our marriage, I hadn't been interested in much more than no-strings sex.

Knowing how small Stolen Hearts Valley was, I avoided getting tangled up with anyone here. That was definitely complicated, and I had no interest in complications.

Usually when Rylie spent a weekend with Melissa's parents, I headed to Asheville. There were always errands to do, and there were always women to find. Women who didn't know my story and wanted nothing more than a few hours of a good time.

Not only was Valentina local, but we also worked at the same place, *and* she was a virgin. Every time I circled back to that, I had two diversionary trains of thought. On the one hand, it was fucking stupid for me to think I was the guy to take care of that. Yet on the other, I couldn't fathom some other guy taking my place. As if it were *my* place to claim.

I didn't realize I was staring at Valentina until Dani cleared her throat. I checked myself, managing not to jerk my head, and casually looked away, keeping my expression bland.

"What's up, Valentina?" Dani asked. "Lucas was just leaving." Her eyes caught mine, and there was a slight gleam in them. Knowing Dani, I knew she'd noticed I might be noticing Valentina. I could easily shake that off. Valentina was just plain gorgeous, like stop-on-the-street-and-stare gorgeous.

And I *was* a man, after all.

I glanced from Dani to Valentina and nodded. "I was. You two have a good day," I said as I turned, unable to resist a last lingering glance at Valentina as I passed by.

Valentina gave off this odd combination of an old soul carrying a sense of innocence and purity. Of course, the knowledge that she was a virgin certainly contributed to that. Yet even before I'd known that about her, I'd noticed she was rather an open book about everything. I wasn't just saying that because she babbled on about why she got herself that hot pink toy. Valentina was just plain nice.

And sexy as sin.

I was about halfway down the hallway adjacent to the lodge kitchen when I heard footsteps behind me, and Dani saying something into her cell phone. She was in a rush to get somewhere, that much was for sure. Not seeing Valentina behind her, I spun back and returned to Dani's office.

Valentina was standing up from a chair when I stepped in the doorway. She turned, saying, "Oh, I thought you had to ..." Her eyes collided with mine, her words trailing off.

Her cheeks flushed pretty and pink, and holy hell, I wanted to kiss her so damn bad it almost hurt.

"Dani ran off, I see."

Valentina nodded. "Yeah, some problem with one of the reservations."

I stepped into the office, resisting the urge to close the

door behind me. If I did that, I wasn't so sure I could keep myself from spreading Valentina out on Dani's desk.

"Did you need something?" she asked, her tongue darting out and sliding across her bottom lip.

Her foot started tapping on the floor. She wore a pair of jeans and a loose T-shirt. Nothing about her outfit was sexy, but when it came to Valentina, she was plain sexy.

"I just need one thing," I heard myself saying.

In two strides, I was standing right in front of her, savoring her scent. That subtle citrusy scent I'd forever associate with her.

"What's that?" she asked, her voice coming out low and husky.

"I thought maybe you'd let me steal a kiss."

Her mouth dropped open in a pretty little O, and her eyes widened. After a moment of dead silence, during which I couldn't get my eyes off her and my breath became short, she nodded.

"I don't think it's stealing." She gasped as I slipped an arm around her waist and pulled her flush against me. I didn't even care that my arousal was obvious, hard and insistent, pressing in the cradle of her hips as I pulled her close.

"Okay then, it's a gift," I murmured, bending low and brushing my lips across the wild flutter of her pulse along the side of her neck. Dusting kisses along her jawline, I made my way to her mouth. Her lips were soft and pliant under mine.

I tried to keep myself in check, tried to hold back, but the moment she sighed, I was lost. Her tongue slipped out to slick against mine. Kissing her was like getting spun into a fire, but it felt so fucking good. She tasted like honey, and her mouth was warm and yielding as I claimed it.

I lost all sense of everything but Valentina. My world narrowed to the feel of her plush body pressed against mine as she arched into me. The soft sounds coming from the back of her throat drove me fucking crazy. On the heels of a gasp with a muffled cry into my mouth, another sound barely punctured the haze of lust filling my mind.

I couldn't resist gliding my tongue against Valentina's just one more time before I forced myself to pull away. Her eyes fluttered open, wide and dark with a desire I knew was reflected in mine. Her lips were puffy and pink, and it was all I could do not to start kissing her all over again.

The sound I now knew to be footsteps drew closer. "Until next time," I said, unable to resist smiling when she curled her hand around the hem of my T-shirt as if to tug me back against her.

She opened her mouth to say something and snapped it shut quickly when Jackson's voice reached us. "Hey Lucas," he called. "Dani said I could find you back here."

"Right here," I replied, taking a quick stride back to place an appropriate distance between Valentina and me.

Jackson leaned into the doorway. "There you are. Hey, Valentina," he said easily, tossing a quick smile her way.

"Hey, Jackson. Shay asked me to meet with Dani to go over the accounts from last month," Valentina explained.

"Of course. I gotta steal Lucas from you."

"Whatcha need?"

"Oh, we got a big load of hay. Wade and Dawson are both out this afternoon, so I figured maybe I could sweet-talk you into helping me out."

"Is this your version of sweet talk?" I quipped.

Jackson rolled his eyes. "I guess it is."

"Sure thing. Give me a few, and I'll meet you out there."

Jackson nodded. "Thanks, man." At that, he spun on his heel and headed back down the hallway.

I liked working for Jackson. For starters, he was a friend. While he was technically everyone's boss here, seeing as he owned the lodge, that wasn't how he approached running the place. He approached it as a team endeavor and worked harder than the rest of us.

He'd only just slowed down a bit in the past few months

because he fell head over heels in love with Shay. I'd known the first day she was here that he would fall in love with her if he hadn't already. It was good to see him relax enough to forget about work sometimes.

I glanced back at Valentina, unable to resist catching her hand in mine and meeting her halfway as I tugged her toward me.

"What are you doing?" she whispered fiercely, her cheeks turning that pretty shade of pink again.

"We have a small problem," I heard myself saying. It felt as if I were always hearing myself say things when it came to Valentina now. My words skipped ahead of my thoughts and danced out of my mouth before I had a chance to check myself. The cylinders in my brain didn't seem to fire on time when it came to her.

"I want to kiss you every time I see you," I murmured right before brushing my lips across hers again. Because I couldn't resist one last touch.

She made another one of those soft sounds in her throat and sighed. I let myself have just a taste, a quick swipe of my tongue against hers before I stepped away, quite reluctantly.

"Is that a problem?" she teased, throwing me off balance.

Even though it had only been the past week or so that I'd let myself think about Valentina this way—as a virgin sexpot—I knew she had a sense of humor. She'd regaled the staff a few times at dinner with funny stories about the contrast of her life with her parents. Prayers morning and evening, and people cutting pills in the church bathroom and selling them to the congregation if they could get away with it.

"Well, I won't say it's a bad idea. Just that I'm guessing you don't want me kissing you in front of everyone."

She shrugged. "Whatever. I don't have many secrets."

I held her gaze for a long moment, the pull to reach for her again magnetic. I resisted the urge and smiled, reaching out to tug on that loose curl resting against her cheek. Her hair was silky in my fingers, the curl bouncing when I let it go.

"Until next time then," I said as I forced my feet to turn and leave. This time, I made it all the way down the hallway. I had Jackson waiting on me.

I stepped out into the bright sunshine, running into a wall of heat. It was August in North Carolina, which meant it was hot as fucking hell. The air was soft, the humidity caressing my skin. Sweat formed almost instantly as I strode down the path that led from this part of the farm to the other.

A cluster of trees and a small rise were between the barns and the old farmhouse. Jackson had built a new barn in this area, which served as the vet clinic upstairs with the horses in the lower floor. Built into a hill, the upper floor had parking for the clinic.

Another new barn sat on the far side of the pasture and housed the rescue program and a hodgepodge of animals. The family's original farmhouse sat across from the vet clinic beside the pasture.

As I walked quickly, Valentina consumed my mind every step of the way. Beyond the heat, I could've used a cold shower just to calm my body down. As it was, I had to force her out of my mind to get my arousal under control. The last thing Jackson needed was to see me worked up.

Chapter Nine

VALENTINA

"So what's up with you and Lucas?" Dani asked a few days later.

A second ago, we had been discussing some new accounts for supplies. She shifted gears so fast I practically got whiplash.

Although it probably would've happened anyway, I blamed my blush on her catching me off guard. I looked up, trying to ignore the fiery heat on my cheeks, but Dani's expression was bland. I might not have known her for long, but I knew better. She was fishing.

"Why would you ask that?" I countered, striving to keep my tone casual.

"Um, because he couldn't keep his eyes off you. And I know that look."

"What look?"

"The one where Lucas looked like he'd have been quite happy if you two were alone in the room, so he could lock the door and have his way with you," Dani explained pointedly.

I leaned back in my chair with a sigh, figuring I might as well not even bother to fake any of this.

"He kissed me," I announced.

A flash of satisfaction pierced me at the look of surprise on Dani's face. "What?!"

"He kissed me," I repeated. "Twice."

"I think I'm going crazy," Dani replied, giving her head a little shake. "Are you serious? Of course you are. I don't even know why I'm asking. You're probably the single most honest person I've ever met."

"Oh, that can't be true. You're totally honest, and Shay's honest and Evie and so on."

Dani picked up a pencil and started twirling it between her fingers. "I don't mean other people are dishonest. Just that, well, you're not even good at faking it."

I could be sly when I wanted, and I chose now. "Oh, like when you pretend you don't have a thing for Wade?"

Dani's eyes narrowed, and the pencil stopped spinning. "Oh, I see how it is. You can be sneaky. Anyway," she continued, sidestepping my comment about Wade, "my point was I observed Lucas noticing *you* in a big way. And now you tell me he kissed you. Next thing I know, I'm gonna walk outside and Gloria will be flying," she said.

I burst out laughing. "Is it that unusual for Lucas to kiss someone?"

Dani placed the pencil back in a mug full of pens and pencils on her desk and cocked her head to the side. "I don't know exactly how unusual it is. What *is* unusual is Lucas doesn't like complications. He's certainly never kissed anyone who works here. Because *that* would be a complication."

Seeing as I'd already blurted out what happened, I decided now was a good time to scope out some info on Lucas. Dani seemed to know just about everything about everyone. "What happened to Rylie's mother?" I asked.

Dani sighed, sadness flickering in her eyes. "She died. Aneurysm."

"Oh my God," I said slowly before quickly gulping in a breath. "That's so sad."

"It is. Rylie had just turned one. As I told you before, it turned out she was having an affair behind Lucas's back with one of his friends."

An abrupt jab of pain hit my chest. Even though I'd already heard that detail, it burned. "I feel kind of angry with her, but she's dead, and that doesn't seem right."

Dani nodded. "Yep, that about sums it up. You just elucidated what Lucas has been dealing with since he found out. It hit him hard. He might not be my type, but Evie's right. You'd have to be blind not to notice he's got it going on. He and Melissa dated in college and were pretty serious, and then she got pregnant. Lucas was so damn excited about that baby. If there's one thing I can tell you about Lucas, it's that when he commits to something, he's all in. That was what he was like with Melissa and Rylie. Of course, he's still like that with Rylie. That man would lay down his life for his little girl. But as far as kissing anyone other than a one-night stand on a weekend out of town, well, let's just say it has *not* happened. I would know." She eyed me, her gaze almost wondering. "Wow."

"Why do you say wow?" I was honestly curious.

"I dunno," Dani finally said after several beats. "You're crazy beautiful, but you keep to yourself in a way. I guess I'm a little shocked because you don't strike me as the kind of woman anyone would think of as casual."

I could see her point. I didn't know what Lucas saw in me.

Now that he'd kissed me—not once but twice—while I might not understand his motivations, I recognized the wild in the pulse of desire between us. I might not have much experience with desire, but I knew what I felt, and it was powerful.

Eyeing Dani, I replied, "I have no idea, but he sure is a good kisser."

Dani burst out laughing, slapping her hand on her desk as she threw her head back. "Oh my God! I love that about you," she said when she managed to stop laughing.

"Love what?"

"You just tell it like it is. It's fucking awesome." Pausing, she narrowed her eyes. "Hey, what are you doing tonight?"

"It's top secret, but I'm not doing anything. I'm just going to my cabin to read. I don't know if you noticed yet, but I don't have a very busy social life."

Dani smiled. "Oh, don't bash yourself for that. Except for Dawson, and here and there Evie and Grace, most of us here work and sleep, and that's about it. I was asking because Shay's coming over to have pizza and wine with me later. I thought maybe you could join us."

"I'd love to."

Dani grinned as she stood from her desk. Perfect. "We'll have to get Shay's opinion on Lucas."

My cheeks heated again, and I rolled my eyes. "You should know I haven't had much practice with girl talk."

Dani shrugged. "Who cares? We're just glad to have you here. I can tell you this, and I'm being dead serious, you are a godsend to Shay and Jackson with the accounting. Ever since Jackson and his sister got this place up and running, they were using this accountant in Asheville. He was fine, but they don't exactly have a straightforward situation here. Between the rescue, the lodge, and the vet clinic, it's complicated. They really needed someone like you to come in and tidy it up."

I beamed. "Oh, I'm so glad! I love this job."

Dani rounded the desk and curled her arm around my shoulders, giving me a squeeze as we walked out of her office and down the hallway.

"I need to get up front to check on some stuff in the kitchen. Shay and I are going to meet here at seven. I'll leave some food out for anybody who's picking up, but I'm not cooking a meal for the staff tonight. We'll see you at seven?"

At my nod, she waved and hurried through the doorway into the kitchen. Meanwhile, I left out the back, intending to return to my cabin and ... Oh, who was I kidding? I was probably not going to get a damn thing done while I mooned over Lucas. God, that man could kiss.

I figured I didn't even need the rest. Kissing alone was enough.

Chapter Ten

VALENTINA

"More wine?" Shay asked from across the table, lifting the bottle and arching a brow.

Glancing at my glass, I shrugged. "Sure. It's not like I'm driving anywhere."

Leaning over, Shay tilted the bottle and filled my glass with more of the deep red wine. Dani returned to the table, sliding a platter straight out of the oven onto the middle of the table and handing out three plates.

"In case I didn't mention it, change of plans. Nachos instead of pizza. I didn't want to miss out on the ripe avocados, which go from ripe to the compost in about an hour, so we had to beat the clock. I've got fresh guac and salsa, so hang on," she said. Spinning away, she walked quickly back to the table in the center of the kitchen, returning with two bowls of the promised additions.

"Dani makes the best nachos," Shay said solemnly.

The heaping platter had tortilla chips layered with melted cheese, fresh tomatoes, sliced onions, and beans. My mouth watered just looking at it.

"I bet she does," I belatedly replied.

Dani chuckled as she sat down. "Shay's just saying that to make sure I keep feeding her."

"No, she's serious," I said with a vigorous nod. "I'm pretty sure you make the best of everything."

Dani's cheeks flushed lightly, and she shrugged. "I love to cook, but y'all don't need to flatter me to make me do it."

Shay rolled her eyes and nudged Dani with her shoulder. "You just told me Valentina is the most honest person you know. If you can't trust the rest of us, at least take her word for it."

Dani twisted her lips before taking a sip of her wine. "Fine. I won't argue the point."

We settled in to enjoy her nachos. After a few bites, Dani glanced at Shay, and asked, "So how are things with you and Jackson? Now that you're not dancing around each other anymore."

Shay's cheeks flushed slightly. She finished chewing, and a smile unfurled slowly. "Well, um, things are great."

Dani caught my eye and winked. "They are *so* in love. It's ridiculous."

"Even I can tell he's head over heels in love with you," I offered. I meant it. Jackson was so obviously enamored with Shay. It was quite sweet really.

"You two deserve it," Dani said, her gaze sobering slightly.

Although Shay never spoke of it, I knew from the news that she'd been through her share of hell. What with her ex ending up splashed all over the news after assaulting her and subsequently killing two people when he was driving drunk.

I knew a bit about the weight of the past. Not that I had my own heavy past to carry. With my parents opening up our church and home to people in need, I had an idea of just how quickly a life could crash and burn as events snowballed out of control. I was glad for Shay's sake that she had landed on her feet after what she went through.

Shay smiled softly. "I don't know that we deserve it any more than anyone else, but I'll take it."

Dani's speculative gaze landed on me. After our conversation earlier that afternoon, I knew she had lingering questions. I sensed she was trying to assess if it was okay for her to mention anything in front of Shay. It was. Due to how managed my childhood had been, the idea of being the subject of gossip almost thrilled me. Although I didn't know if it counted as gossip when it was just between three people, and I was one of them.

I glanced at Shay. "Lucas kissed me."

She almost choked on her sip of wine, her eyes widening.

Dani started laughing. She handed Shay a napkin to wipe up the drop of wine running down her chin. "Yep. I was shocked too."

"You already know about this?" Shay asked before shaking her head. "Oh, I don't even know why I asked. You know everything before anyone else does."

"Hey, I only found out today," Dani protested. "And only because Lucas couldn't keep his eyes off Valentina."

Shay cast a wondering glance in my direction. "I don't know what to think."

"Yeah, me neither," Dani not-so-helpfully added.

After pausing to add a spoonful of guacamole to the nachos on her plate, Shay looked over. "So I'm guessing you like him?"

"Of course. What's not to like?" I replied, striving to keep my tone casual.

It was a wasted effort because my cheeks were flaming. I didn't even know how to describe how I felt about Lucas. My body felt like a hot fizzy drink inside when he was near. Odd, but that was how it felt.

"He pretty much keeps to himself," Shay commented, glancing at Dani. "What do you know?"

"Everything I told Valentina earlier. As far as I know, Lucas hasn't dated anyone since his wife died. He *definitely* doesn't like complications. If I had a little more nerve, I'd ask him about Valentina."

"Wow," Shay said, her tone deadpan. "*You're* short on nerve? That's a new one."

Dani rolled her eyes before her gaze swung to me. "Okay, now that we're not busy, how did this whole thing start anyway?"

My cheeks got even hotter. "Here's what happened. He accidentally got a package for me," I began.

"What the hell was in the package?" Dani interjected.

"Exactly what I was wondering," Shay chimed in.

Embarrassment aside, I figured I might as well tell them the truth because it was kind of funny. I also needed some advice. "A vibrator," I replied with a sheepish smile.

This time, Dani spit out her wine. Shay burst out laughing, snagging a napkin from the stack in the center of the table and handing it to Dani.

"Oh my God! Did he know what it was?" Dani asked as she wiped the wine off the table.

"Unfortunately, yes," I said with a sigh. "The box just had the lodge address on it."

Dani bit her lip to keep from laughing again. "Did you just want to die?"

"Pretty much, but it's a good story."

"So he kissed you then?" Shay asked, tapping her fingers on the table as she nibbled on a tortilla chip.

"No, not then. He kissed me the other night when I brought Rylie out to his truck after she spent the afternoon with us at the clinic. She was sound asleep," I explained.

Shay grinned. "Don't worry, the world wouldn't have ended if she'd been awake and he kissed you."

"I know, but still. Anyway, then he kissed me again today. Now I don't know what to think."

"I think Lucas really likes you," Dani said, her curls bouncing as she nodded emphatically.

I was quiet, absorbing that observation. The thing was, I

didn't really know how to interpret any of this. I knew the authenticity of what I felt between us. My one concern was his daughter, but we didn't have to let any of this affect Rylie. It never crossed my mind that Lucas would want anything more from me than something sexual. I couldn't say why I thought that, but it seemed the least complicated option. For a man who didn't appreciate complications, that is.

After a few beats, I shrugged. "I don't know. It was just two kisses. Maybe that's all it will be."

Somehow, I wasn't quite ready to tell them he told me he'd be at the lodge for the upcoming weekend and just what the implications of that might be.

"Whatever you do, be careful," Shay said, her gaze sobering.

"Careful?" I asked in return.

"There's always Rylie to consider—for him and for you."

I left dinner later with that comment lingering in my mind.

Not that I had romantic aspirations. But that certainly drove the point home that nothing was simple in this situation.

Chapter Eleven

LUCAS

My eyes tracked the peanut butter as I smeared it on a slice of bread, then quickly moved onto the next. I had four peanut butter and jelly sandwiches to prep. That was Rylie's request for her weekend with her grandparents. Not that she needed the peanut butter and jelly sandwiches made by me—Betsy and Dale, Melissa's parents, certainly fed her quite well—but Rylie claimed I made the best ones ever, so here I was making them.

Major bonus to being a father—feeling like a superhero for small tasks.

Because Betsy and Dale adored her, they would humor her and let her have her sandwiches for lunch every day. I questioned the wisdom of preparing sandwiches for four days, but I imagined peanut butter and jelly could survive a nuclear holocaust.

Betsy and Dale had found out about Melissa's affair only recently and not from me. I had mixed feelings about them knowing. For starters, I preferred my privacy. While I wasn't the one who had the affair, people knowing about it meant questions for me. I had hoped it had been long enough that perhaps they would never find out, but Stolen Hearts Valley was a small area, and secrets rarely stayed hidden for long.

I only knew they knew because Betty called me. She had apologized on behalf of her daughter and left me speechless. I mean, what the hell was I supposed to say?

It was long over, and Melissa was dead. Jade's comment last week tumbled through my mind. It was hard to imagine making room for an actual relationship in my life. There was Rylie to consider. I had *no* idea how single parents navigated the landmines of dating with a child in the equation.

Valentina loomed in my mind—her wide blue eyes and her riot of red curls. She was a walking contradiction. Everything about her screamed sex to me, and she was a fucking virgin.

Actually, that wasn't quite right. She didn't scream just sex. Even before I had noticed her in that way, I'd noticed she was kind and generous around the lodge, always offering to help. She was also funny and unintentionally blunt.

I hadn't forgotten how well she had done with Rylie during her impromptu babysitting duties. That fact burned in my thoughts.

Rylie referred to her as Valentine, which made me laugh. Rylie insisted I ask for some shredded paper for her "hay" for her toy horses. When I'd asked where she got that idea, I learned it had come from Valentina.

Thinking about Valentina and Rylie made my mind go in directions it shouldn't. I did *not* need to be thinking about Valentina like that. I needed to keep her clearly compartmentalized so the lines didn't blur. Because beginning tomorrow, I'd be staying at the lodge for four days.

The problem with trying to keep Valentina compartmentalized was she kept sneaking all over the place in my mind. It had all been fine and good after that rather surreal encounter when I returned her package. Oh, I wouldn't lie, I had wanted her so fiercely ever since that afternoon, and I intended to see it through.

It had been easy to manage when I told myself it was just lust.

Then she had to go and be so damn natural with Rylie. Ever since Melissa died, it was just Rylie and me. I'd sworn off trying to bother with dating because it was too complicated, and it required me to trust. I considered it easier to stay single and leave dating entirely out of the equation.

But with sexy as sin Valentina dancing through my dreams and getting me so damn hard with her kisses, I couldn't get her out of my mind.

It hadn't occurred to me that she might be at the vet clinic when I stopped by. Logically, I should've considered that, seeing as her office was there.

Rylie had mentioned Valentina almost daily since she spent the day with her and Shay. She loved meeting new people, so that wasn't exactly a surprise. But now, for crying out loud, here I was imagining Valentina as something more than the hottest little sexpot. She had burrowed her way into my brain and body.

Desire was a funny thing. When I was young, like most guys, lust ran hard and fast. It was purely hormones driving the boat, so to speak.

When Melissa and I started getting serious, I had settled into it easily. We were seniors in college then. We got an apartment together and both started working.

Sex wasn't as wild as it had once been between us, but we got it on pretty regularly. By the time she got pregnant, we'd been living together for three years. Melissa was my only serious relationship. We got married, and I felt truly committed. I never doubted it.

That first year after Rylie was born was a blur. Between work and raising a baby, we didn't talk much, but then I didn't have much time to talk. I never minded taking care of Rylie even when I was tired to the bone. I wouldn't pretend it was always easy because that would be bullshit. But it didn't chafe on me, not at all.

I gave my head a shake as I finished assembling the peanut butter and jelly sandwiches. It was late, and Rylie was in bed. I put each sandwich in an individual bag and stacked them inside a plastic container. The container sat beside her to-go bag, a rather large bag with a giant pig on the front. After she encountered Gloria and Squeaky at the rescue, Rylie fell in love with pigs. My mom had even sewed her a stuffed pig because she was crafty like that.

My throat tightened with emotion for a beat. Rylie might have lost her mother, but she was loved hard.

With thoughts of Valentina spinning through my mind once again, I walked into the living room. Nights were quiet here. After Rylie went to bed, I usually flicked through the channels and watched whatever show caught my interest. Sometimes I read. Sometimes I wondered—because my nosy sister had to bring it up—if my nights would always be this quiet.

That night, I lay in bed, realizing I hadn't actually fallen asleep with a woman since Melissa died.

Chapter Twelve

VALENTINA

I clicked through the spreadsheet, smiling when the numbers added up to what I expected. When I went to college, I didn't know what I wanted to do, yet I had always loved math. Something about the certainty of it soothed me.

Between being homeschooled and having parents who were religious in an earthy sort of way, kind of flaky, and ready to save the world at the same time, well, it had all added up to me not fitting into any category too easily while I was growing up. I'd spent most of my life feeling out of place, so perhaps that was why I found certainty so comforting.

Back to the numbers. Math was one area where I felt comfortable, and it came easily to me. I blew through my undergrad requirements. When my advisor suggested accounting as a major, I didn't even hesitate and was accepted into an accelerated master's program.

Even after I walked away with a degree that made me easily employable, I promptly agreed to handle the accounting for my parents' church and retreat programs. The hardest part about taking the job at Stolen Hearts

Lodge was telling my parents and quitting my job working for them.

I was three months into my new job, and I still loved it. There was a knock on my door, and when I glanced up, Shay stepped in. "We're about to head out. You're all set with dealing with the animals, right?" she asked with a smile.

"All set," I replied as I tapped save and closed my laptop.

"Thanks again for helping with that," she said as she slipped into the chair across from my desk. She reached up to tighten her ponytail, cocking her head to the side as she dropped her hands. "Well, have some fun this weekend. Maybe you could actually go out to Lost Deer Bar with everybody else. Dawson said that's where everyone's planning to go."

"I might," I replied.

"Either way, have a good weekend," she said. She stood just as Jackson appeared in the doorway, leaning against the frame with one hand in his pocket.

"Ready to go?" he asked, his gaze lingering on Shay.

I wondered if I would ever have a man look at me the way he looked at her. I felt as if I'd abruptly interrupted an intimate moment by witnessing the depth of emotion contained in his gaze. Knowing what she'd been through, I was so glad to see them together.

"Ready," Shay said, turning to face him with a smile.

Only then did Jackson glance my way. "Thanks for taking care of the animals. If you need anything, just call us, okay?"

"Of course. I can't imagine I'll need anything."

"By the way, I asked Lucas to help you with the horses. We just took in a new rescue today that's a bit of a handful. Lucas said he'd be over at the barn this afternoon by five. Wait for him, okay?"

"Sure."

Shay shook her head. "You just had to agree to take that stallion. I told you he would be wild," she said, her lips tightening and her gaze bouncing back and forth between us.

"That's why Lucas is going to help," Jackson replied smoothly.

Just thinking about Lucas set my body to humming and my belly spinning in a quick flip. I could hardly stop recalling the feel of his lips against mine the other day and his promise about this weekend. I didn't know quite what it meant, but I knew I couldn't wait.

———

Early that evening, I crossed the pasture to the rescue barn. Gloria came ambling along behind me. I heard her before I saw her because she made a soft snuffling sound whenever she approached people. Glancing behind me, I couldn't help but smile. Gloria was a giant mostly white pig with a few dark spots. She was sweet as could be, and it felt as if she knew exactly what I was saying when I talked to her. It was something about the way she studied me with her careful expression.

"Hey Gloria," I called, pausing to wait for her to catch up to me. She stopped at my side, nudging my knee with her nose as we began walking together.

She followed me into the barn, and I paused to look around. The dogs were on one side with the rest of the animals on the other. Each dog had its own door to exit into a large play yard. Most of the dogs were rescues with the exception of one who had become a permanent resident—a sweet English Setter named Pepper. She played with the other dogs during the day and stayed at the farmhouse with Jackson and Shay at night. For this weekend, she was staying out here in the kennel because they thought she would be most comfortable here while they were gone.

On the other side was a large stall for two goats and the stall Gloria and Squeaky shared. They generally came and went as they pleased. There were also chickens in a large coop outside with their own space.

After taking care of all the other animals, I fed Gloria and was wondering where Squeaky was when she announced her presence with a few squeaks. As soon as I made sure she was fed, I glanced at my watch and realized Lucas was probably already waiting at the horse barn for me.

Closing up, I ran across the pasture, pushing through the door and feeling breathless as I came through. Lucas was there, leaning against one of the stalls about halfway down the aisle. He was stroking the new stallion's neck. When I heard the low murmur of Lucas's voice, the sound sent a hot shiver through me.

Ignoring it, I approached. "Sorry I'm late."

Lucas said something softly to the horse, his hand still resting on the horse's neck. The horse was tall with a rich brown coat and a black tail and mane. Lucas and the horse turned at once. Both of them had such intense eyes, my heart started racing. The horse eyed me curiously for a moment but quickly lost interest, turning to nibble on some hay in a netted bag hanging inside the stall.

Lucas's attention, on the other hand, didn't waver. His green eyes met mine and swept up and down my body. My skin tingled all over, heat flashed through me, and butterflies took flight in my belly.

"I didn't know you were supposed to meet me at a certain time, so there's nothing to apologize for," he said. "The horses are all taken care of."

For a moment, I was unable to form a word. My mouth seemed to run at two speeds with Lucas—nothing or verbal diarrhea.

"Oh," I finally said. "Jackson told me he asked you to come help me. He was worried about the new stallion." I gestured to the horse behind Lucas.

"Right. He's all taken care of."

The barn was quiet. As I stood there, a humming electricity began to spin through me.

"Okay. Well, thank you," I replied, my words coming out a little choppy.

Lucas pushed away from the stall, taking a few strides before stopping in front of me. He wore jeans, the denim so soft the fabric molded to his muscular thighs. My eyes lingered on the flex of his forearm when he slid his hand in one pocket.

My mouth wet dry, and my pulse rocketed to the point I could hardly catch my breath.

I felt more than saw his eyes sweep down my body again. My outfit was rather nondescript—a pair of leggings with a baggy T-shirt. I probably smelled like animals at this point. Nothing more than the heat of Lucas's gaze made my skin prickle and my belly flip.

"Are you done for the day?" he asked.

The soft sound of horses chewing their hay surrounded us as we stood there. The barn was cool, a contrast to the heat of the humid August evening.

Swallowing, I nodded. "Uh-huh."

Lucas stepped a little closer, reaching out and catching one of my hands in his. He smelled like hay and sweat and Lucas, a scent I had come to identify with him—musky and warm with a slight woodsy hint.

His thumb brushed across the back of my hand, and all my attention narrowed to the feel of his calloused pad moving back and forth. The touch was subtle, and he probably wasn't even thinking about it, but it was electrifying.

"I want to kiss you now," he said, his words sending a hot thrill up my spine.

I licked my lips and swallowed again, barely able to get a breath in. "Please do," I finally murmured.

I wasn't consciously trying to whisper, yet this moment felt so heavy, so intense. It felt as if at any minute, sound would snap it to pieces.

His lips kicked up at one corner. Every smile he gave me,

even a half of one like this, made it feel as if the sun was breaking through on a cloudy, gray day.

Lucas didn't smile much. And now that I knew more of his history, I understood why.

"I might want to, but I won't. We'll have to save it for later," he replied.

"Why?" My question flew out on its own in a rather demanding tone.

That half smile stretched to the other corner of his mouth. "Because the guys invited me to go to the Lost Deer Bar. Seeing as I'm here for the weekend, and it's what I would usually do, it's best if I go."

"Oh, well, I'll probably go too then because Shay mentioned it earlier."

Still smiling, Lucas glanced away as if gathering his thoughts and shook his head with a low chuckle. His eyes made their way back to me. "Well then, I suppose you should go. It'll be a special form of torture for me."

"Torture?" I queried.

Lucas arched a brow. "Valentina, I don't think you know how much I want you," he said flatly.

His words sent another thrill through me. "Oh," I managed. My body felt buzzy, tingling all over.

My hand was still in his. He turned then, giving me a gentle tug. "Come on. I'll drive."

Chapter Thirteen

LUCAS

Lost Deer Bar had been around for decades. Once upon a time, it was probably small, but this little bar in an old log cabin tucked in the hills of the Blue Ridge Mountains had expanded quite a bit since its origination sometime in the 1950s.

According to the story, the bar was named as such because the couple who founded it had gone out for a drive because their daughter thought a deer was lost. As if there were such a thing. I supposed deer did get lost—maybe—but the likelihood that a little girl would somehow know that was slim.

That said, if Rylie wanted me to go out for a drive to search for a lost deer, I would do it. Honestly, I wouldn't even hesitate. Whether or not we found it, I would come up with a story that made her feel better if she was worried about it.

Back on that drive, the couple passed by the old home and noticed the For Sale sign. That started the ball rolling for what would eventually become the Lost Deer Bar. The one-room log cabin still had the original bar on the side, but all they had back there were memorabilia and old photographs. It was now the entryway to the massive rectangular room with a bar running along the back wall and tables scattered throughout. One corner had pool tables and mostly card games. It was busy most nights. Being only a few hours shy of Nashville across the border in Tennessee, they also had music often with fledgling new bands passing through here on their way to fortune and fame.

The décor was simple. There was wide plank hardwood flooring worn from years and years of feet passing over it, and circular wooden tables with booths to match. They were open from five a.m. until two a.m. Aside from the bar, they served all three meals and had delicious, simple fare.

I was keeping to one beer for the evening since I was driving. As I had told Valentina back in the barn when it had taken just about all of my discipline not to kiss her, tonight was a special form of torture for me.

I only offered her a ride because that was generally how things were among the staff and friends at Stolen Hearts Lodge. Knowing most everyone else had already left, either Valentina and I showed up together, or Dani would give me a hard time for not offering her a ride.

Not that I minded giving her a ride. That said, I was starting to question my restraint and endurance. She sat beside me, her wild red curls barely tamed in a ponytail where they were half falling out. I wanted to reach over and pull that elastic out so I could watch her hair fall loose before I buried my hands in it.

I knew I was half insane. I did *not* need to be taking things further with Valentina, but damn if I could stop myself. Not to mention, every time I considered it, I reminded myself that Valentina was looking for something, and she would find it. I'd be damned if I let some asshole take advantage of her.

Aren't you taking advantage of her?

My skeptical mind threw that question out. My answer was swift. *Hell no.*

And exactly how do you know you're the man for that? My skeptical mind was quick to counter.

My experience with virginity was limited to a girlfriend back in high school. For what it's worth, I was a bit of a fumbling idiot, though we still had fun.

As for now, I told myself plenty of experience would stand me a good stead. I'd left my sanity in the rearview mirror. It wasn't even a speck anymore.

I sat at the table beside Valentina, the sexiest woman I had ever laid eyes on, enduring her coaxing allure. She tempted me just by being there.

"Jesus, Wade, sometimes you have such a stick up your ass," Dani sniped at Wade who sat at an angle across from me.

Wade rolled his eyes and drummed his fingers on the table. "I do *not* have a stick up my ass, Dani Love," Wade drawled. "You're giving me shit for worrying about my little sister?"

Dani nodded vigorously, her brown curls bouncing. "Yes, I am. She's a grown woman. Her boyfriend might be kind of dumb, but then ..." Her words trailed off with a sharp laugh. "All right, you might have a point."

My mouth almost fell open. Dani and Wade tended to snap at each other over just about anything. They'd known each other forever, and as far as I knew, once upon a time, they almost dated. It was short-lived and ended with a big argument where Dani stormed off and threw her slushy at him in the high school cafeteria.

I heard Valentina say something under her breath, and I leaned over. "What was that?"

She grinned, a teasing glint in her eyes. "I said they need to get over it and do something about it."

I chuckled. "Right? We all know that, but they've been at this for years."

Valentina shrugged and leaned forward to pick up her margarita. My eyes honed in on the sight of her tongue tracing over the salt along the rim of the glass. I was suddenly envious of that damn glass.

Fuck me. I tore my eyes away only to collide with Wade's gaze. Dani had already moved on and was saying something to someone else. Meanwhile, Wade appeared to have a front row seat to me lusting after Valentina.

He winked and grinned. Knowing Wade as well as I did, I imagined he would give me shit about it at some point. Wade was a good friend, the best kind of friend really.

He had the unfortunate, decidedly awkward role of filling me in on what he eventually learned about Melissa and Seth. Although I had stumbled across the evidence in Melissa's texts on my own, plenty of gossip was skittering through Stolen Hearts Valley like leaves in the wind. When Wade heard about it, bless his damn heart, he scouted up the gossip and shut it down. He also punched Seth.

I hadn't asked him to take it to that level and certainly could've done it myself. I just hadn't quite felt like it. Still didn't. For me, Melissa was responsible for the betrayal, and she was dead.

I returned Wade's grin with a shrug, letting myself get tugged into a conversation about the schedule for the construction of more guest cabins at the lodge.

I forced myself not to simply stare at Valentina, and for the most part, I think I managed it. I wasn't the most chatty guy, never had been, and I thought I had my response to her under control until she decided to play a game of pool. There wasn't anything particularly unusual about that. I flicked through my memory bank and tried to recall if Valentina had ever joined in a game of pool when I was here with friends, but I couldn't recall any.

But then, beyond noticing she was fucking hot as hell, I'd made a concerted effort not to pay too much attention to her before. Now, she'd grabbed my attention so hard it just wouldn't let go.

All because of that package.

I found myself leaning against the wall by the pool table.

"Sweet shot," Dawson said with a low whistle.

I hadn't noticed where the ball went. Not with Valentina bent over and her sweet bottom on display. For me. Or so my body thought. Between our encounter in the barn and driving over here, she had showered and changed. She wore a skirt, nothing particularly revealing, but with a smoking body like hers, everything was a tease.

Summer in the Blue Ridge Mountains meant the heat wrapped itself around you and held on. I abruptly thought she needed more clothes on. Her skirt was some cotton stretchy thing that fell to her knees in a little twirl. Atop that, she wore a loose T-shirt. Unfortunately, I vividly recalled just how her breasts felt against me, so I knew what was hidden under there.

The sound of someone clearing their throat nudged into my awareness, and I tore my eyes away from Valentina's delectable ass to find Wade standing beside me, leaning on his pool stick. "Nice view?" he asked, his tone deadpan.

"Shut up," I muttered.

Wade chuckled. "Nah, not going to shut up. Far as I'm concerned, it's nice to see you noticing anyone."

I caught his eyes and rolled mine in return.

Valentina straightened, smiling over at Dawson. She lifted a hand and tucked a curl behind her ear. It didn't skip my notice that Dawson took a nice long look at Valentina.

An irrational bolt of possessiveness struck me, demonstrating precisely why I'd lost my damn mind.

Dawson was a friend, and most of the time, I had nothing against his predilection for playing the field. Dawson liked a good time, and he never led anyone on. Yet Valentina deserved better.

"Chill, dude," Wade said from my side.

I slid my eyes to him. "Since when are you my keeper?"

"Since you look like you want to kick Dawson's ass just for noticing Valentina is hot. He won't lay a hand on her. She's hot, but she's totally not his type. Too damn innocent."

I almost groaned aloud. If only Wade knew the half of it. Before Valentina told me, I might've thought she threw off a hint of innocence—because she did—but I'd never have guessed she was a fucking virgin.

The tension bundled up inside me, the result of me trying to keep my body in check for hours, eased slightly. Because Wade was right. Dawson went for party girls. While Valentina clearly could hold her own in a game of pool and didn't shy away from a few drinks, she was no party girl.

I sighed. "I know."

Dani conveniently distracted Wade from giving me more shit. She started up with him about some order they needed to take care of. With Dani running the lodge restaurant and Wade helping Jackson mostly run the outdoor adventure scheduling, those two, fortunately or unfortunately depending on how you looked at it, bumped into each other enough to rub each other the wrong way.

If not for the fact I had abruptly decided to get the hell out of there, I could've waited to call him on his own bull-shit. As it was, I didn't think it was a smart plan for me to hang tight and wrangle with feeling possessive over Valentina.

I paid my tab and made sure to cover Valentina's. I was torn at the moment. I could easily leave and let her know to catch a ride back with someone else, but that didn't feel quite right. Not to mention, even if I was half out of my mind, I was at the end of my tether with her.

Chapter Fourteen

VALENTINA

I leaned my head back to look at the sky just outside my cabin. The heat from the day still held the night air in its grip. Although the nights were cooler, cool was a relative term when some days had over ninety percent humidity. The air was so laden with moisture it slammed into you when you stepped outside. I loved the night air because it was soft and held the fading scent of flowers.

Lucas stood beside me, his presence quiet. My pulse had been running wild ever since we left the bar. I was trying to catch my breath, but all I could manage were shallow gulps of air.

The stars were bright in the night sky with the moon peeking out from behind wispy clouds drifting through the darkness. After taking a shaky breath, which did absolutely nothing to slow my thundering pulse, I brought my gaze down and let my eyes slide sideways to Lucas.

We had stopped in the trees between the parking area and the winding path to where the staff cabins were scattered. I idly wondered where Lucas stayed when he spent a weekend here.

I learned from Dani, who was ever helpful, that when Jackson was gone, Lucas often stayed on for the weekend to help manage everything. Between the guests, the various adventure trips, and the first responder work, there was no shortage of things to do.

He'd been quiet on the drive back from the bar. But then, Lucas was usually quiet, and for the most part, quiet didn't bother me. Yet, just now, I was unsettled with my body revving like an engine. I wanted to ask a million questions.

I was restless and anxious, but not in a bad way. I was ready to get this over with. When I looked his way, heat flared in the air between us. His eyes dipped down, the feel of his gaze akin to a flame flickering over the surface of my skin.

All we had for illumination was the soft, silvery light of the moon filtering through the trees. Through the darkness, the small light on my porch glowed ahead.

Lucas turned, stepping closer and reaching for one of my hands. I didn't even hesitate. I was happy to just hand myself over to him, which was insane really. I trusted him completely, and I didn't know why.

Well, that wasn't quite true. Jackson and Shay trusted him, and so did Dani. I knew he was a good man. After seeing him with Rylie, my heart cracked open a little because he adored her so clearly. It was downright endearing to see the look of love on his usually stark and somber face when he looked at his daughter.

While growing up with my funky parents who loved me and had their own unique view of the world, my mama had told me to save myself for the right man, for a man who I knew would love me.

Somehow, I knew that Lucas was the right man even though love had nothing to do with it. I'd wager Lucas had no intention of loving me or any other woman. After hearing what happened, I surmised he was a guarded man with good reason.

That was completely okay with me. I didn't need to be head over heels in love. I just needed to do something with all the sensation and emotion spinning through my body. With the way I felt the two times he kissed me, I had complete faith this would be about as good as it could get.

When the pad of his thumb brushed across the back of my hand, the slightly calloused surface was rough against my skin. I was surprised I didn't melt like butter—given the humidity of the night and the fire that burned inside whenever he was close.

I looked up at him, watching as his gaze coasted over my face. I didn't know what thoughts were passing through his mind, but I was suddenly impatient. I needed something concrete, something to hold onto.

So I stepped closer, resting my palm on his chest as I leaned up on my tiptoes, meaning to kiss him. His mouth kicked up at one corner, and my belly felt funny, all shivery and hot, and almost ticklish.

Before I could ask him what was funny, he said, "You are something else, Valentina."

"What do you mean?" I asked, my question coming out a little raspy.

I was close enough to feel the hardness of his body. He was all muscle, every inch of him. With my palm resting on the muscled plane of his chest and my eyes trailing over his corded arms, I knew, I just knew, I couldn't wait to see him bare.

"You should be nervous, and you're not," he said softly. "I feel like I should warn you."

"No, you should kiss me."

Lucas's mouth kicked up at the other corner. His hand tightened around mine to tug me a little closer as his other hand glided down my spine, his touch a blazing a path of heat through my T-shirt.

"As you wish, darlin'," he murmured as he bent low. He paused when his lips were but a whisper from mine. "You sure?"

That brief pause sent my pulse into the stratosphere. I felt as if my entire body was leaning toward something, teetering on the edge of a cliff, about to leap forward and fly. I wouldn't fall. I knew that. Because Lucas was just the kind of man to catch me.

He waited while my heart pounded and blood rushed through my ears. I realized he was waiting for me to actually answer. *Sweet Jesus.*

"Yes!"

Just when I wanted him to rush, to dive into this and treat it like the race my body thought it was, he did the exact opposite. His lips brushed across mine once and then twice. He dropped a kiss at one corner of my mouth and then the other. His arm wrapped securely around me, pulling me close and holding me tight against him. He was so strong, so steady.

I felt as if I might spiral out of control and quite likely would've, yet he would be there to keep me from spinning loose. Only after I gasped did he fit his mouth over mine and thread his hand into my hair. He swept his tongue into my mouth, capturing my moan in our kiss.

With the moon shining down from above, Lucas kissed me as if I were the center of his universe. I lost all sense of time and place. My senses were firing with a multi-faceted focus—Lucas, the feel of his mouth, the soft prickle of his beard, the strength of his embrace, and the utter decadence of his hard-muscled body against mine.

I'd never been so hyper aware of my softness. Everywhere I was soft, he was hard. My breasts pressed against his chest, and I felt the curve of my bottom under his hand as he palmed my ass.

I have no idea how long he kissed me in the trees in the hot, sticky summer night. He tasted decadent, a hint of mint mingling with his musky scent. I wanted to eat him up, to have all of him to myself—my own personal playground.

However long that kiss lasted, when he broke free, I instantly felt myself leaning forward as if scrambling for more. He cupped my nape and leaned his head back. His body was taut, his heart beating hard like a drum. I could feel it pounding along with my own wild heartbeat.

He murmured something indecipherable.

"What?" I asked.

"Let's get inside," he replied, his tone tense, bordering on something that sounded like anger.

I didn't know how to interpret it. Because I was me and I never hesitated to ask questions, out stumbled a question. "Are you upset?"

Lucas was easing his hold. I'd been on my tippy toes with no weight on my feet as he held me against him. He stepped back slightly, one hand catching mine and the other sliding down my shoulder and arm, his thumb pausing at my elbow and tracing over the soft skin there.

Every touch made me hyper aware of areas on my body I never thought much about. For example, that tiny strip of skin where my elbow bent was insanely sensitive to his touch, little streaks of fire racing away and butterflies taking flight to spin wildly in my belly.

I tried to catch my breath, but my lungs weren't having it, and I was barely able to get in more than a shallow gasp.

"Oh no," he said, his tone low and intent. "I'm far from upset, Valentina. It's just you make a man crazy."

I searched his face, watching as his eyes softened. Without another word, he turned, striding swiftly along the path with my hand held in his strong grip, the pine needles crunching under our footfalls.

Chapter Fifteen

VALENTINA

Within minutes, we were in my small cabin, the contrast of the cool air sending goose bumps chasing over my skin. We were smack dab in the middle of some of the hottest days of summer. The August heat could be oppressive even after the sun slipped below the horizon.

The cabins here were far from rustic. They were small, but they were all connected to central air. During daylight, they were bright and airy with sunshine falling through the windows. A light pine ceiling that angled high above gave the studio room a sense of space. There was a bed, a small bench, and a dresser.

The tiny kitchen at the corner had just enough room for a small refrigerator, a microwave, and a coffeemaker. I hardly ever used it, but in a pinch, it would do. My luxurious bathroom was the biggest bathroom I'd had in my life. My parents were solidly middle class, so I had shared a bedroom and bathroom with my little sister, always cluttered with towels and the mess we made.

At the sound of the door clicking shut, I turned to find Lucas right there. I hadn't thought through this part because

I had no experience to go on. Just when I started to get anxious and wonder what I should do, he caught my hand and reeled me right back into the kiss from moments ago.

This time, his hands roamed over my body as he nearly drove me out of my mind with nothing more than a kiss. Though I didn't have much to compare it to, I suspected very few kisses could measure up to one from Lucas.

His kiss was a mix of slow and fast, soft and hard with deep sweeps of his tongue as his mouth worked over mine masterfully. All the while, pinwheels of heat spun like fire through my body. My knees went weak as sensation rushed over me.

He read my body like a book, and before my knees collapsed, he lifted me, turning and setting me on the bed, one of those tall four-poster beds. He slid my hips onto it, then stepped back.

Just now I noticed I'd somehow kicked my shoes off, catching sight of them out of the corner of my eye. Sensation stole my breath, my pulse thundered out of control, and the butterflies in my belly fluttered, distracting me. An insistent neediness gathered inside, rolling into itself, the force intensifying.

I didn't even notice when I rubbed my thighs together in a futile effort to ease the pressure building there. I could feel the slick moisture between my legs, and my panties were wet with my arousal.

"Oh now, darlin', you're gonna kill me," Lucas said as he stepped between my knees, trailing his finger down the side of my neck and along my collarbone to dip down into the valley between my breasts. Oh, how I wanted that finger to keep on moving. His touch was a blaze of fire, and my nipples were so tight they ached.

Unfortunately, he stopped, the pad of his finger pressing right there between my breasts. My entire body was vibrating from that one tiny spot.

"Don't stop!" I burst out.

I got one of those delicious smiles from him. It was small and sly, and oh my God, it made me rub my thighs together again.

His gaze darkened. "God help me," he murmured as his hand dropped down. The backs of his fingers grazed one of my tight nipples before he caught the hem of my T-shirt, pulling it up and over my head in one smooth move.

The air was cool on my skin, the contrast only heightening the heat building inside. With my skin slightly damp from the humidity outside and the cool air conditioning in here, my skin prickled.

Looking up, I watched his eyes sweep over me and linger on my breasts. My bra was dark navy silk to match my navy T-shirt. I wasn't much for worrying about what I wore and tended to go for comfort, but I preferred nice underwear. It was a small thing I did for myself. With Lucas's gaze on me, I realized perhaps it wasn't just for me.

My T-shirt had fallen into a pile on the floor beside the bed, and I wanted his to join it. Just as I reached for the hem of his shirt, he flicked his thumb on the clasp of my bra. My nipples puckered tightly. With a shake of my shoulders, my bra slid down my arms. He tugged it free and tossed it to the floor to join my shirt.

The air around us felt heavy, nearly vibrating from my anticipation and desire. My sex clenched, and I became acutely aware of the slick heat at my core. I wanted to rub my thighs together again to ease the ache there, but I couldn't, not with him standing between them.

"So here's the thing," he began as he lifted a hand to cup my chin, his thumb tracing slowly along the edge of my jaw. "You follow my lead. Think you can handle that?"

A hot thrill shot through me, zinging like electricity straight to my core. There was something so decadent about him being a little bossy. Part of me wanted to surrender to it while another part of me wanted to push back, to ask questions, to demand.

Although I was mostly an obedient girl growing up, that was my downfall—always getting in trouble for asking too many questions and pushing back and talking when I was expected to be quiet.

His thumb circled my lips, and my tongue darted out to taste him. His eyes narrowed, and his mouth kicked up at the corner. "I think you might wanna argue with me about that," he said softly, his slow drawl sending my belly into a flip.

I shrugged, feeling my skin tingle and my nipples tighten with him so close. "Maybe," I finally said.

His low chuckle sent another wash of heat over my skin. "You do that, darlin'," he replied just before he brought his mouth to mine again, his hand sliding into my hair, gripping lightly as he angled my head to the side.

The brush of his beard against my cheek was yet another sensation tangling up with the others. The subtle tickle nearly undid me.

This kiss took things to another level entirely—hot, wet strokes of his tongue against mine as he devoured my mouth. By the time his lips broke free from mine, I was gasping for air as his tongue blazed a hot, wet path down the side of my neck. One of his hands slid down my spine to cup my bottom. He tugged my hips to the edge of the bed as he stepped a little closer.

My skirt had ridden up around my hips. I whimpered when I felt the hard ridge of his arousal through the denim of his jeans pressing against the thin silk of my panties. I could hardly focus with streaks of fire racing through my body. I felt awash in need, tumbling and stumbling from it. I wanted to pay attention to every touch, yet I was so intoxicated by him I couldn't focus on anything. His other hand lifted, the backs of his fingers trailing over the curve of my belly to cup one of my breasts, his thumb brushing back and forth across the aching peak.

A flickering corner of my mind was barely conscious and

aware I was about to get caught in the undertow of the desire rushing between us. Once that happened, there would be no stopping it. This was all too much, all too good.

He dipped his head, his mouth closing over a nipple. The pleasure was piercing, and I cried out as he drew away. The cool air hitting my damp skin tightened my nipples even further. I could hardly take it.

Lucas lifted his head from where he was tracing his tongue over my collarbone. Who knew my collarbone was an erotic zone? Certainly not me.

I was beginning to wonder, however, if it was Lucas who made everything so amazing. It seemed he could touch me anywhere, and I melted like butter in his hands. My pulse was skittering wildly, and my breath was coming in sharp pants.

"You are so fucking beautiful," he muttered, his low, dark, and rough tone making my pussy clench.

When I dragged my eyes open, I found his hungry gaze on me. My heart gave a hard kick, and I felt funny inside again as if I were falling from a great height.

When he cupped my bare breast in his palm, I arched into his touch with a whimper. "That's it," he murmured, his lips landing on my skin like a hot brand.

His tongue teased in the sensitive spot just above my collarbone and trailed down between my breasts. I gripped the sheets and comforter with one hand and tangled my fingers in his hair with the other. Raspy sounds came from the back of my throat, my entire body tightening as sensation streaked through me.

His fingers teased the soft curves under my breasts. Finally, *finally*, his mouth closed over my nipple, sucking lightly as I gasped in relief. He practically tortured me with his lips and tongue. After he had one drawn so tight it hurt, he switched his mouth to the other. The brush of his beard against the sensitive skin—a hint of a tickle—only intensified the other sensations pinging through me. I held onto his shaggy curls, my hips rocking into his arousal. I was desperate for release.

I might've been a virgin, but I was no virgin to orgasms. Yet with a mere two teasing encounters with Lucas seared into my memory, and now this one where everything was pushing past boundaries I'd never crossed, I was abruptly learning I had no idea just how fierce the edge of need could burn. He had yet to even touch me right where I wanted him to touch me so desperately, and I was toeing the edge of release already. Every nerve in my body was on fire.

"Lucas, please ..." I gasped, ready to beg.

He stilled, drawing away, his teeth grazing over a nipple as he lifted his head. My hand fell from his hair as he traced his thumb in lazy circles through the moisture left behind. "Yes?"

It took an effort to open my eyes. While my heartbeat galloped, and I was at the edge of my willpower, shredded with pleasure, he looked calm in contrast. The only giveaway was the subtle rock of his hips into the cradle of mine, the hot length of his arousal pressing hard against me. That, and the heat banked in his gaze.

"Hurry," I gasped when he rocked into me again.

His features were almost severe in the shadowy room with nothing other than a lamp on in the corner. He shook his head slowly, his thumb circling my nipple again. "Oh no, darlin'. We're not rushing."

I let out a huff, and his eyes took on a gleam. "Impatient, aren't you?"

I rolled my eyes and slid a palm up under his shirt because I *needed* to feel his skin. A flash of satisfaction rolled through me when his breath hissed through his teeth. I thought he might stop me, but he didn't. His skin was warm and smooth. I slid my palm up over the ridges of his abdomen. I'd heard of such a thing as six-packs, but I'd never felt one.

My fingers encountered a light dusting of hair as I made

my way up over the planes of his chest. His shirt bunched along my wrist, and I sighed when I exposed his chest. With a muttered curse, he reached behind his head, yanking his T-shirt up and over in one quick motion where it fell to the floor beside mine.

My mouth went dry. Just as I had suspected, he was a work of art, his bronzed skin tight over nothing but muscle. The dusting of black hair only illuminating his raw masculinity.

Lucas's body was beautiful, to put it bluntly. But not in the sense of someone who spent much time thinking about it. He worked a demanding job and lived a demanding life. His body was a reflection of both.

I leaned forward, stringing kisses over his muscled abdomen, before he murmured, "Fuck, Valentina, slow down."

"I ..."

His mouth cut off my words when he leaned over me, partially covering my body. The entire surface of my skin tingled as streaks of fire shimmered under the surface. He shifted his weight slightly, so he was still resting between my thighs but not all of his weight was bearing down over me. I found I wanted the heaviness and his strength to surround me.

The dusting of his hair on his chest tickled my breasts and had me arching up to feel more. He simply kept kissing me. Once again, I lost myself in the madness with his mouth working over mine.

He threaded a hand in my hair, roughly cupping my nape as he angled my head to better feast on my mouth. With my skirt bunched around my hips, I savored the rough feel of the denim on the insides of my thighs as I curled my legs around his waist and rocked into him. I wanted him. So, so much.

Sensation was pinging through me, sparks flying, my heart thudding, and blood rushing through my ears. I was frantic with need. I slid a hand down his back to cup his ass when he rocked into me yet again, his hard cock pressing against my clit and sending sweet, piercing streaks of pleasure through me.

Lucas was moving, his lips blazing a trail down my neck, between the valley of my breasts, and dallying briefly at my nipples. His lips dropped kisses over my belly as he pushed my knees apart. He murmured something against my skin, and I cried out in protest when he rose up. He ignored me, lifting my hips, and yanking my skirt and panties off all at once.

He paused to look at me, the mattress dipping slightly under his weight. I could feel the heat of his gaze, my skin tightening everywhere, my belly and core clenching. I barely even noticed this was the first time I had ever been entirely naked in front of a man.

Somehow, what might've made me feel vulnerable didn't. Not with Lucas. Although I had no illusions. I didn't think he was going to sweep me off to some kind of silly love and happily ever after. He was a good man. There was something about him—the way he looked at me, the way I felt with him—that spun into what I knew about him as a man. I felt utterly safe with him.

And needy, oh so needy. I rested on my elbows. "Come here," I demanded, shifting my legs.

His low laughter sent need radiating from my core. "So impatient."

I opened my mouth to tell him to take his jeans off. Because I *was* downright impatient to see what lay behind there. My words caught in a gasp when his hands glided up my thighs, slowly pressing my knees apart.

On the burgeoning list of sensations I had never considered, the feel of his calloused palms on my skin was oh, so hot. As I was trying to absorb that with heat chasing in the wake of his touch, my belly tightening, and my sex clenching, he dipped his head and pressed his lips to the soft skin at the bend in my knee.

Another brand-new erotic zone discovered. I murmured something, falling back onto the pillows as his lips trailed up my thigh and he settled his shoulders between my knees. His beard tickled my skin, the feeling spinning into all the others.

In my planning, prior to tonight, which had comprised years of curiosity, I certainly knew about this possibility. I was a little uncertain as to the results. Fact number one: I had never experienced oral sex—giving or receiving. Fact number two: while I didn't know what to expect, I had heard the results varied.

But then, from my understanding, all results were largely variable when it came to sex. As far as I could gather, women usually got the short end of the stick.

So far, Lucas was obliterating any lingering doubts. His fingers teased over my slick folds where I was so wet. I felt rather than saw him draw back. When I looked down, he was lifting his head languidly, his eyes dark. There was something erotic about the sight of him with his face right there in front of the most private part of me.

His fingers shifted again, sliding inside me. My head fell back as I cried out, arching into it. I had so many questions, and all of them fled from my consciousness. His tongue licked me just as another finger joined the first. I basically lost my mind, cast into the sea of pleasure.

I gasped and whimpered with my hips rocking into his touch. He was thorough, exploring with his fingers and tongue. I was right there, so close to the edge of release. I had never teetered on the precipice like this for so long. I was fisting the sheets, pleading with him, when he finally swirled his tongue, driving his fingers deeply into my channel before sucking my clit lightly into his mouth.

Pleasure detonated inside me, flattening me and rolling through me in hard, crashing waves. Lucas stayed with me, my channel clenching and throbbing around his fingers. I was just starting to catch my breath when I felt him slowly rise.

Opening my eyes, I met his gaze. He looked almost as if he were in pain, his features taut. One hand rested on my thigh, his fingers damp with my arousal.

My pussy clenched again, and I reached for him. Despite my sated state and feeling like liquid, I wanted more. I flicked the buttons to his fly undone in a second.

And discovered he was commando. Oh, yes. His cock sprang free, long, hard, and thick. I leaned forward, wanting to taste him just as he tasted me.

"Val ..."

My name ended in a ragged groan when I swirled my tongue around the tip of his cock.

Chapter Sixteen

LUCAS

My control was under assault, hanging by a frayed thread, and it was about to snap. Seeing Valentina with her lips swollen from our kisses and her red hair a wild tangle around her face as she swiped a drop of pre-cum off the head of my cock with her tongue, nearly undid me right then.

I shackled myself, calling upon discipline I didn't even know if I had, and tried to step back. "Tonight's just for you."

Her wide blue eyes stared back at me. The freckles on her cheeks stood out when she was flushed. There were freckles everywhere, and I wanted to kiss every single one. I would have to save that for later.

I promised myself, for no sane reason whatsoever, that I wasn't going to just fuck Valentina tonight. That would come later.

With her gaze on me, she shook her head. "That's not fair."

Uncertain what to say, I leaned down and fit my mouth over hers, cupping one of her breasts lightly. I almost groaned at the feel of the round, soft weight in my hand, her nipple ruched tight as I rolled my thumb over it.

I fisted my cock, stroking it once, twice, and then again, my release spurting between us over my hand and onto her gorgeous, freckled belly.

A sound of protest came from the back of her throat before she pulled away. "No!" She twisted her lips, her eyes narrowing as she looked at me.

"Next time," I said softly.

"Promise?"

"I promise," I heard myself saying, distantly wondering if I'd flat-out lost my mind.

Well, I suppose I didn't need to wonder, not with the evidence of my release on Valentina and the taste of her on my tongue.

I eased away from the bed, striding into the bathroom. With a quick glance around, I found a clean washcloth on the shelves above the toilet. I meant to dampen it and bring it to clean her up, but she appeared in the mirror behind me as I was running the hot water.

If I thought Valentina was dangerous for my sanity before, I had no idea what I might be forced to face when I saw Valentina naked with her skin flushed all over and her eyes flashing. In all honesty, I hadn't expected her to be shy because that just wasn't her personality. She might be quiet at times, but not shy. Shutting off the water and buttoning my jeans, I turned to face her.

She cocked her head to the side and rested a hand on her hip. "Are you leaving?"

"Not just yet."

She pressed her finger to the center of my chest, that one tiny dot of contact sending a sizzle of electricity through me. My cock twitched. Considering I'd just come all over her, that was saying something about the power of my body's response to her.

"Lucas," she began before faltering, uncertainty flickering

through her gaze. "Is it because I'm not experienced enough?"

My mouth actually fell open. "Hell no, Valentina. No." I shook my head hard as I curled the damp washcloth in my hand, feeling it cool. Turning, I flicked the faucet on again, dipping the washcloth under the warm water quickly and wringing it out. Turning back, I wiped my cum off her belly. She was quiet, biting her lip and watching me.

As I scrambled for purchase in my mind, I knew the problem was I wanted her too damn much. I didn't want to just fuck her. I wanted to make love to her, so she would never forget it and never want another man for the rest of her life.

That was fucking insane.

A part of me that was comfortable in a certain place—comfortable with distance and keeping anything that elicited my emotions at bay—wanted to play it cool and simply shrug. But I couldn't do that to Valentina. She was too authentic for me to degrade that.

After I tossed the washcloth in the sink, my eyes snagged on the robe hanging on the door behind her. Reaching past her, I caught it in my hands and drew it over her shoulders. She looked at me like I was crazy, and frankly, I was.

Next thing I knew, I was pulling her into my arms and burying my head in her hair, breathing in her scent. It was as if somehow I needed her to anchor me. None of this made sense. She should be the anxious one. I wasn't a nervous wreck about the sex, not at all. In fact, I was acutely aware Valentina was seared permanently into my heart, body, and soul. Here I was, hoping to ruin her for all of the rest, but the script had flipped. She had ruined me for all the other women.

No one would ever come close. *Ever.* And we hadn't even had sex, for fuck's sake.

I couldn't let tonight go any further because I had to prove to myself I had *some* control. Even if it wasn't much.

This rampaging need for her was slipping out of my grasp, and I couldn't let that happen.

"No," I muttered into her hair. "You're not too inexperienced. That has nothing to do with this. Maybe I'm fucking crazy, but I don't think it's right for this to be a one and done thing. You know what I mean?"

I felt her lean back and forced myself to lift my head even as I knew that looking into her eyes was risky. My heart banged against my ribs. I wanted to stay right here and bury myself in her sweet heat and sleep beside her.

"I know what one and done means," she said, catching her bottom lip in her teeth again and nibbling on it, promptly redirecting my blood to my groin.

As it was, I'd be returning to where I usually stayed upstairs in the offices and have no choice but to take care of matters by myself.

"Tomorrow night," I said, knowing I couldn't offer any further explanation. "I promise."

"Promise?"

"I promise."

To my immense relief, she tied the belt on her robe and stepped out of the bathroom. Turning back to face the mirror, I rinsed the washcloth again and laid it on the side of the tub.

I took a long look in the mirror. My eyes were dark, my hair messy, and my skin slightly flushed. A man teetering at the threshold of his control stared back at me.

Chapter Seventeen

LUCAS

I tugged the silencers off my ears, flicking the switch to turn off the miter saw. After setting the silencers down on the table behind me, I leaned against it, snagging a cold bottle of water out of the cooler to one side and lifting my T-shirt to wipe the sweat off my brow.

Hot or not, we had work to do. Jackson had plans for four additional guest cabins. With the adventure lodge staying busy all the time, Jackson was wisely adjusting to that by expanding the guest lodging bit by bit every year.

Today, I was working with Wade and Dawson on a cabin. We were laying hardwood flooring, and somehow, I'd ended up on duty for cutting the wood. We needed the miter saw for the angles and corners. Jackson had pulled me aside and asked me to mostly run these projects when he wasn't around. Dawson and Wade were plenty capable when it came to building, but they weren't much for the more detailed work.

Jackson liked things to look good. Among other things in my life besides my first responder work and work as an adventure guide here, I'd worked with a construction company during the summers when I was in college. The money was good, and I didn't mind the hard work. My father was also a builder, so I'd learned a ton from him.

In working at Stolen Hearts Lodge, Jackson set the tone. There was no top dog jostling for space bullshit. Everybody had their strengths, and Dawson and Wade were perfectly happy to help me run the show for this kind of project.

The rhythmic sound of the pneumatic nail gun stopped when Dawson put in the last board for this room downstairs. He straightened, setting the tool on the floor, and turned to stride across the room and lean against the table beside me.

"Hand me a water, would you?" he asked as he dragged the hem of his T-shirt across his face.

Snagging a cold bottle, I tossed it to him. He rolled it across his forehead, letting out a sigh. "It's fucking hot, man," he offered.

"Tell me about it."

He chuckled just as Wade came down the stairs. "I could use some water too," Wade said as he crossed the room toward us. When I tossed it to him, it slipped free from his grip, the condensation on the bottle making it slick. Leaning over, he chuckled as he fetched it off the floor. He sank down onto a nearby crate. "Can't believe it, but we're ahead of schedule. If we push, we can finish this one before Jackson gets back. What do y'all say?"

I took a few swallows of the ice-cold water and nodded. "I'm in. I'm here all weekend, so let's bang this thing out."

Dawson looked back and forth between us and rolled his eyes. "You two ever think about fun first?"

Wade's gaze met mine with a wink. "Lucas usually doesn't. I can't say I ever do."

Dawson rolled his head to the side, sliding his gaze to me as a sly grin stretched across his face. "Oh yeah, I think for Valentina he might consider some fun."

I bit the inside of my cheek, resisting the urge to tell him to fuck off. I stayed quiet while Wade grinned. "No sense in trying to keep secrets around here. Evie asked me if you two had something going on last night."

Although I was in the hot seat at the moment, I didn't miss Dawson's too alert gaze when Wade mentioned Evie's name. Dawson was a player. He was a good guy, but he had a rotating door in his bedroom or, rather, in the bedrooms of women around town.

I wasn't much for gossip, but I was plenty observant, and it hadn't escaped my notice that Evie was in a category of her own when it came to Dawson. Oh, he teased her, and he flirted with her, but the man flirted with everybody. However, his interest seemed a notch higher than usual with her. She also knew how to get under his skin.

After another swig of water, I noticed two expectant pairs of eyes waiting. "I don't have a thing going on with Valentina," I said with a sigh.

That was a blatant lie, but I damn sure didn't feel like chatting with anyone about Valentina and me. It felt too private, and I couldn't even think straight when it came to her. I made no bones about the fact I had no intention of getting serious. All the guys knew Rylie was my priority. All the guys also knew I found ways to get my needs met when the urge got too strong. But those ways were practical, no strings, and certainly didn't involve anyone I worked with.

Dawson swung his eyes back to me, his gaze disbelieving. "If you say so. But I know how that girl looks at you, and we sure aren't blind either. Don't get me wrong, she is *seriously* easy on the eyes, so I definitely don't blame you for looking a little too long."

Wade chuckled, and I was relieved he let it drop. I was friends with Dawson, and he was a damn good guy. As much as he teased, he was solid as a rock out on calls as a first responder, though I didn't have a friendship with him the way I did with Wade. I knew Wade knew my interest in Valentina was more than fleeting.

Conveniently, Dawson's phone blared out several sharp

buzzes. "Gotta take this, guys. Speaking of women, I have a date tonight."

He tossed his now empty bottle of water in the recycling bin in the corner and strode out the open front door. Wade took a long drag of his water before lowering the bottle and holding my gaze. "All right, man, it's none of my damn business, but I'm just gonna say one thing."

"Just one?" I countered, my tone dry.

In reply, his tone was dry as dead grass. "I know you have priorities. Well, mainly one—Rylie. And I get it, man. She's your daughter, and her mom is dead. She's got you, your family, and the rest of us. But this thing with you acting like you are *never* going to give another woman a chance? It's fucking stupid, man."

I opened my mouth, about to make some bullshit cutting remark about him, but he silenced me with a look. "I'm sure you're tempted to give me some shit, but save it for another day. I'm trying to be your friend. If something is up with you and Valentina, that's none of anybody's damn business. My point isn't really about her because that's not what I'm talking about right now. If the right person comes along, Rylie could have another mother. Mothers take every shape and form. She'll always have Melissa, but Melissa's gone. You know I was adopted and for the very same reason after my mom died. The only mother I remember is the one I have. And thank fucking God my dad gave her a shot."

I wanted to point out that, as far as I knew, his birth mother hadn't screwed around on his dad behind his back. But that wasn't his point, and it sure as hell didn't matter today.

My throat tightened, and I paused to drain the bottle of water, swallowing right through the pain. "I get your point, man," I finally said. "I guess we'll just see what happens."

Wade looked surprised at my reply.

I laughed. "I *do* get your point."

He stood, kicking the crate away as he did. "Hot damn,

maybe Valentina is the one. It's going on four. As far as I'm concerned, let's call it a day since we're ahead of schedule as it is, and we can start early tomorrow before it gets too hot. You cool with that?" he asked.

"Absolutely. I've had my fill of being hot and sweaty."

———

Hours later, I was once again tortured by Valentina's presence. Per Jackson's request, I'd gone over again to take care of the horses. I hoped—even if I didn't want to admit it to myself—to have a few minutes alone with Valentina.

No such luck. Evie was there, chattering away the whole time, as she tended to do. Wade stopped over to let me know a load of hay would be delivered tomorrow as well. I went from that little crowd to an even bigger crowd over dinner at the lodge.

With it being the weekend, Dani was busy managing the restaurant and the evening meals there. As she often did, she managed to throw something together for the staff. No matter what she made, it was delicious. Tonight, she had made a cucumber salad paired with fresh cornbread and macaroni and cheese with ham.

Whether it was deliberate or not, when I approached the picnic table at the back of the kitchen, Wade scooted over to make room for me beside Valentina. Because that was what I needed—to have her scent drifting up to me, and the feel of her body warm and soft beside mine.

I didn't trust myself not to lay a hand on her, no matter how deep the temptation ran. I could feel her thigh brush mine. Of course, when I looked her direction, I had a rather excellent view down the V of her T-shirt. Fuck me.

Ryan was sharing a story about a kayaking trip earlier that ended with him in the river tugging out two sopping wet college women. He scrubbed his hand in his hair and shook his head. "I swear to God, I get so tired of people not buckling their life jackets. It's a simple enough thing."

Dawson winked. "Ha, wish I'd been in charge of that trip."

Evie pursed her lips and cast him a glare. "Is there any situation you don't take advantage of?"

"Not that I know of, sweetheart," he replied with a sly grin.

Ryan chuckled and paused to take a sip of his beer. Wade interjected, deftly moving the topic onto something else. "So, Evie, are the rumors true about Mack?"

Evie cast a bright smile at Wade and nodded. "Yup. He's moving back sometime after this fall. I can't wait."

"I don't think I've met Mack," Dawson added. "He's your older brother, right?"

"He sure is," Evie replied.

Valentina paused to sip her wine. "I don't think I've met Mack."

"Well, you didn't go to school with us," Evie offered. "You were homeschooled, right?"

Valentina sighed. "Yes. It was kind of lonely. Wish I'd known y'all growing up. The only kids I knew were the ones who went to my parents' church."

I marveled at that detail. Although I didn't think Valentina was a wild girl, as evidenced by her still virgin state, I imagined it chafed at her to be sheltered like that when her personality was so open and curious.

Grace Lakes, who only occasionally joined us for dinners, cast a wide-eyed glance at Valentina. "Really?"

Valentina nodded, brushing a loose curl off her cheek. "It was okay. Life is what it is. Don't go thinking my parents were too strict. They were in some ways but not in others. They were recovering hippies who fell in love with Jesus and wanted to homeschool me because they didn't think the public education system was good enough. As it was, I passed all my high school testing exams by the time I was seventeen and went to college early."

"Even though I went to public school, my parents were crazy strict. Yours at least sound a little nicer than mine," Evie commented.

Valentina shrugged, and just then, Dani poked her head through the swinging doors that led into another section of the kitchen. "Grace, you mind starting a little early tonight? It's already nuts out there," she called.

"Give me a few, and I'll be right there," Grace called in return.

The conversation shifted after that interruption, and as the dinner gathering broke up gradually, Valentina's nearness continued to torture me. Part of me was tempted to take a rain check. Not because I actually wanted to, but because I thought I was tempting fate in a dangerous way.

I wanted Valentina *way* too much.

As people filtered out, I stood from the table with the pretense of going to the bathroom. Entering the men's room, I closed the door behind me and leaned against it, taking in a gulp of air.

The subtle flush that crested Valentina's cheeks lingered in my thoughts. I kept telling myself I could keep this compartmentalized, but I liked Valentina. *Too damn much.*

No matter how hard my rational brain tried to tell me this was a bad idea, there was no way in hell I was putting on the brakes tonight.

Chapter Eighteen

VALENTINA

I was seriously annoyed. When Lucas didn't reappear from the bathroom, it became obvious he didn't intend to come back and had slipped out the back, so I decided to head back to my cabin. I'd been lingering and waiting like an idiot.

When we were close to each other, that hum started up between us as if we were caught in an electrical current of our own making. Yet it was clear to me that Lucas had shifted gears back to the way he used to treat me—quiet and hardly ever looking in my direction.

I supposed I could be grateful for last night, but most of me was beyond disappointed. Because somehow, I sensed it wasn't usually so easy. Every touch from him was so decadent, the pleasure cresting so high, I felt as if I'd been floating in the aftermath.

Slipping out the door, I stepped into the warm, humid evening and cut across the stretch of lawn behind the lodge into the trees to the path that led to my cabin. Twilight was falling, stealing the day for the night. The last lingering rays of the hot summer sun faded to a white gold above the mountains, that famous blue gaze barely shimmering in the smudgy sky.

I loved how the sky faded from violet to blue over the mountains at dusk. It seemed magical. I walked up the small rise in the trees, and I could hear a nearby stream bubbling. It was just warm enough that my skin was damp. Twisting a bracelet on my wrist, I took several deep breaths. I didn't like the way I felt—rejected.

My heart stung a little. Like a tiny cut across the surface, just enough to make me wonder if maybe I wanted a bit more from Lucas in ways I hadn't allowed myself to consider. No matter. I needed to forget about him.

Angling through the trees, I paused beside an opening, gazing at the moon over a mountain ridge in the distance. It was nothing more than a curved slice of light in the sky. An owl called in the trees, and I heard the heavy sound of its wings in the air as it flew by.

Turning, I picked my way along the path in the darkness. Moments later, I looked ahead toward my cabin, and my breath caught in my throat. My pulse immediately lunged, and I stopped so abruptly I was surprised my feet didn't actually skid on the pine needles.

Lucas stood on my porch with a shoulder leaning against one of the supports. On the small porch, he was a strong presence in the darkness. He was looking off to the side and turned when a startled squeak escaped me.

My heart felt as if a kite had tugged it hard, yanking it upward and leaving me breathless. I watched as Lucas stepped off the porch, walking toward me. I felt as if I were being pulled by a string, my feet just started moving until I stopped right in front of him.

"I thought you broke your promise," I said.

I hadn't even considered my words, but I'd been thinking I wished he hadn't promised me anything.

Lucas's eyes widened. "Jesus, Valentina. I had no idea where the hell you went. You had me worried."

I stared up at him, sensing he was legitimately worried. "Where would I go?"

His brows hitched up. "Well, I came out of the bathroom, and you were gone. I figured I could catch up to you in a hot second, but you weren't on the path. Did you go somewhere else before you came back here?"

"I just cut over to the view there on the hill, right through the trees," I explained, gesturing vaguely in the direction. I was spinning inside, secretly thrilled he'd been worried.

"How about not scaring me like that again?"

Annoyance flashed inside. "Scaring you? You hardly talked to me at dinner and wouldn't even look at me. Plus, it's maybe two minutes through the trees. I don't see what the big deal is."

"Okay, let's start with that," he returned. "It's dark, and we're in the woods, right at the edge of a big ole chunk of wilderness. There are plenty of snakes around for you to step on, you might come across a bear or ..."

I burst out laughing. Because it was *that* ridiculous. "Oh, my God! You have got to be kidding me. I am perfectly fine, Lucas. Now that you can see that with your very own eyes, why don't you tell me why you wouldn't even look at me at dinner?" I asked, resting a hand on my hip.

He leaned his head back, his shoulders rising and falling with a deep breath. When he leveled his gaze with mine again, my skin prickled all over. My nipples tightened, my sex clenched, and my belly executed a little flip.

Oh. My.

"Valentina, I was not purposely ignoring you. I was trying to keep myself in check. In case you missed the memo, you're fucking gorgeous, the kind of gorgeous that makes men a little crazy. Me, in particular."

Stepping closer, he reached for my hand. I didn't know what I expected, but I didn't expect him to place it over the hard, hot length of his arousal. "This," he said, the word coming out dark and heavy, weighted with something, "is what I've been dealing with ever since I sat down beside you at dinner."

"Oh."

I couldn't help it. I curled my palm over the length of him and slid my hand up and down lightly.

His breath hissed through his teeth. "Dammit, woman. You are going to fucking kill me." At that, he yanked my hand away, holding it fast in his as he turned, pulling me swiftly behind him.

We stumbled into my cabin. Lucas kicked the door shut behind us, spinning me around. My back bumped against the door right before his lips collided with mine.

He had kissed me enough that I thought I had a sense of what his kisses were like. This kiss took everything to an entirely new level.

He devoured my mouth. This kiss was commanding, demanding, and left me reeling. It spun me so forcefully into the desire between us I thought my heart might pound its way out of my chest.

We broke apart roughly, both of us gulping in the air. Plastered against me, Lucas had every hard inch of him pressing into my softness. His eyes met mine, the dark desire in his gaze sending my belly into a free fall.

He closed his eyes for a moment. With his chest pressed to mine, I felt the rise and fall of his breath. When he opened his eyes again, his gaze was almost pained.

His voice was low and hot when he spoke. "Here's the thing, Valentina. I want you. I'd like to fuck you right here, right now against this door. But you need to know that all you have to do is say the word and it stops. At any point. Do you understand?"

One of his hands cupped my cheek, his thumb tracing my jawline. I couldn't imagine why he would think I would want to stop *any* of this, yet I sensed it was important to him that I understand. I could barely think through the blood rushing through my ears with every beat of my heart. I managed a shallow breath.

"I understand," I whispered.

The stark tension in the lines of his face eased slightly. He took another breath before taking a step back. I instantly missed the feel of him pressed against me. There was something simultaneously overpowering and protective about him.

I loved it.

Sliding a hand down over my shoulder, he caught one of my hands in his and tugged me away from the door. As we stood at the foot of the bed, I wondered how to get from this to whatever was next.

I suddenly remembered the mortifying chain of events that set this into motion. My hot pink vibrator. It was still sitting in the top drawer of my dresser. The Bible my mother had given me was in the bottom drawer, safely quarantined from the vibrator.

Impatient, I reached for him. Leaning forward, I dropped kisses along the side of his neck, and I thought he might let me have my way—my way being to hurry things along and get to the good stuff.

But, oh no. He gave me a moment, loosening his grip on the reins of this encounter just enough for me to drag my tongue along the salty skin of his neck.

He threaded his hand in my hair, his fingers cupping my nape. He exerted just enough pressure to force me to lift my head and look at him.

"Not yet," he said gruffly.

In all my life, I never paid much attention to the way a man's voice sounded or how it made me feel. Perhaps that was because no man had *ever* made me feel the way Lucas did. When his voice had that slightly roughened edge to it, the timbre low and deep, it sent shivers chasing over the surface of my skin.

I was about to ask a question, but he shut me right up with a kiss. I didn't mind that. Not at all.

Lucas could kiss me forever.

He angled my head to the side and stepped closer, his other hand gliding down my back in a path of burning heat. He cupped my bottom, his arousal rocking into me as he held me tight against him.

I moaned into our kiss, and he tore his lips from mine, almost savagely. I didn't hear what he said because his lips were on my skin, but I was pretty sure he growled my name.

I forgot everything—everything but the feeling of him surrounding me. His hands mapped my body as his lips teased me with kisses on my neck, trailing over my collarbone into the little dip at the base of my throat, and back to my mouth.

He drew back, tracing along the V of my T-shirt, cupping a breast lightly as he watched me. I couldn't help but clench my thighs together, anything to ease the throb there.

Stepping back slightly, he lifted the hem of my T-shirt, his hands sliding up my sides. "Arms up," he murmured.

I obeyed immediately, a little thrill skittering through me when I saw his mouth curl up slightly at one corner. My T-shirt fell to the floor. Without a word, he flicked the clasp between my breasts. I shimmied my shoulders, my bra sliding off and falling to the floor. I wanted him to touch my bare skin, but he didn't. Not yet.

He hooked his hands over the stretchy waistband of my skirt, dragging it over my hips slowly. He deftly caught the edges of my panties, bringing them down over my legs where they fell with my skirt in a rumple at my ankles.

I looked down, and a little giggle escaped. I was naked, save for a pair of blue tennis shoes and socks to match. When I looked up, I found Lucas smiling slightly. At the sight of his smile, my belly spun in flips.

Chapter Nineteen

VALENTINA

Lucas crouched at my feet, bending on one knee. As I looked down at his dark, mussed hair, he deftly untied my shoes. I stepped out of each one and kicked them loose to the side along with my skirt and panties. I didn't know if he forgot about my socks or just didn't care, but he straightened swiftly. He stopped and stared at me for a moment, the heat of his gaze making my entire skin flush. I was so wet, the insides of my thighs were damp.

I wanted to see him.

To touch him.

To *feel* him.

Stepping closer, I curled my hand around the hem of his shirt and drew it up. He reached behind his neck and yanked his shirt off, slinging it to the floor behind him.

I sighed in delight, dipping my head and dropping a kiss in the center of his chest. I wanted to eat him up, but he didn't give me a chance. Once again, he took control of the situation.

He lifted me with ease, sliding my hips onto the bed and smoothly pushing my knees apart to stand between them.

Then, his lips were on mine again. He tugged my hips to the edge of the mattress and trailed his fingers through my drenched folds.

Meanwhile, his lips made their way from my mouth to my earlobe, sending a hot shiver through me, and down along my shoulder to capture one of my nipples in the warm suction of his mouth. As he teased my nipples, he sank one finger and then another into my channel.

I was breathless, awash in sensation with my hips rocking into his touch and my fingers tangling in his hair. I fell back on one palm, arching into him as his lips mapped their way across my abdomen. I felt the tickle of his beard on the inside of my thighs, a hot kiss on the hypersensitive skin there, and then his tongue licking through my folds.

I was nearly incoherent, gasping, occasionally murmuring his name, and pleading. He didn't draw it out too long tonight. He fucked me deeply with his fingers, his tongue swirling around my clit before he gave it a gentle suck. Pleasure struck me, a sharp, hot, piercing brand right there at my core before it scattered through me.

When he rose, I whimpered because I didn't want this to stop. *Ever.*

The weight of dragging my eyes open took an effort. My belly clenched tight, need boiling inside again at the look on his face. Dark and intent, he seared me with his gaze, and my mouth went dry. The lamp in the corner cast a soft glow on his bronzed skin. His fingers were damp from the juices of my arousal. I could feel them where they rested on my hip.

"So fucking hot," he murmured.

I tore at the buttons on his jeans. His cock sprang free, a pearly white bead dripping from the tip. I wanted to taste it, so I did. Leaning forward, I caught it with my tongue. I glanced up through my eyelashes, expecting him to have something to say. I might not be an expert, far from it, but I already knew he liked to control the pace.

His eyes were on me, the rapid rise and fall of his chest, giving me a little thrill of power. I could tell he was controlled, his fingers tensing slightly where they rested on me.

Shifting closer, I swirled my tongue around the tip, a sense of satisfaction rolling through me when his breath hissed through his teeth. Then he took control. *Again.*

"Not now. Your sexy mouth is going to make me forget my promise." The intent contained in his words sent another wash of heat through me.

He stepped back, and I watched as he reached in his rear pocket, flicking out his wallet and a condom. Everything happened quickly as anticipation coiled so tightly inside, and I thought I might burst into flames.

After kicking his jeans off, he rolled on the condom in no time. The mattress dipped with his weight as he stretched out beside me, lifting me farther up on the bed until the pillows were cool against my shoulders. Although little after-shocks from my climax were still rippling through me, antic-ipation and need were already building inside again like a tide rolling in and out.

As he came against me, his skin was hot and slightly damp. His features were cast in shadow as he brushed my hair away from my face. I was restless, rolling against him and stringing kisses everywhere my mouth could land.

With practiced ease, he took the reins out of my hands by pressing my knees apart. With his lips on mine, I was tumbling right back into the swirl of sensation.

He stilled, and I opened my eyes. I was about to protest, but he beat me to it. "Now would be the time for you to let me know if you want to stop."

I shook my head sharply. "No," I said forcefully.

His eyes searched my face, so I clarified my answer for good measure. "Don't stop."

His mouth kicked up at a corner, and he closed his eyes briefly before dipping his head and dropping hot kisses just behind my ear. His weight came fully over me, his hips settling into the cradle of mine. My body acted on instinct, my knees shifting open wider, inviting him in. I ached to the point of desperation. I *needed* him to fill me.

I felt his cock slide against my folds. He was long and hard—velvet steel. My hips rocked into him, and I let out a little gasp when he slid over my clit, still so sensitive from my climax.

"Tell me if I go too fast," he said, lifting his head briefly from where he had been teasing one of my nipples.

I was so overtaken with sensation that I couldn't even track where his touch was. It felt as if he surrounded me completely in a shimmering web of desire and pleasure.

I nodded my head jerkily, my eyes falling closed on a whimper when he rocked his hips into me again. He barely shifted between my knees, adjusting the angle of his hips. I felt the thick crown of him press into me as he moved at a controlled pace. He sank into me slowly, inch by inch. At first, the sensation was one of pressure. And then, there was a subtle burn. My body went tight, and Lucas froze. I felt him looking at me, but I couldn't even open my eyes.

"Too much?" he asked.

I didn't want to wait and rocked into him. There was a sharp, stinging pain as he was suddenly inside me, filling me completely.

I opened my eyes to find his concerned gaze staring back at me. "Valentina, are you ...?"

His question trailed to nothing when I shook my head. "I'm fine," I insisted.

After several deep breaths, I felt myself relaxing around him. It did hurt, but I was also completely fine. That sensation of fullness was profound. Even through the pain, it was what my body wanted. It slaked the pressure multiplying and intensifying in my core. He held still.

The soft sound of our breaths soothed me. I could feel his heart pounding, hard and fast, against mine. After another moment, my hips shifted restlessly. Every nerve ending felt as if it were on fire. Arching up, I pressed kisses along his collarbone. He leaned down briefly and caught my lips in a kiss, his tongue slicking against mine before he drew back, his head falling into the dip of my shoulder.

I loved the feel of him filling me, the stretch and burn of it, and his weight over me. I felt encompassed by him—his strength and his raw masculinity banging up against his quiet tenderness

Chapter Twenty

LUCAS

Sheathed inside Valentina's slick, tight, hot core, it was all I could do to go slow. She felt so damn good. Her hips shifted restlessly under me. She'd torn the doors off my heart. Every step of the way, she took the edge, pushing a little farther, again and again.

"Valentina," I choked out, "hold still."

"I can't," she said, the low moan coming from the back of her throat nearly undoing me.

I breathed in the scent of her, along the side of her neck, savoring the feel of her skin under my lips.

My cock was so hard it physically hurt. The next time she arched into me, I drew back slowly, expecting her to tense up again. She did slightly, but she flexed into me. The slide back inside her was delicious.

"You feel so fucking good," I murmured, my voice slurred. If it was possible to be intoxicated on desire, I was.

I was supposed to be the one with experience. Hell, I knew I was jaded. I was cynical.

Yet here I was, brought to my knees in every way by a

virgin. The depth of her response to me, her artlessness, slayed me. I'd had enough experience to know I was ruined.

With her red curls framing her face, her soft skin sliding against mine, and both of us sticky from the heat, I was drowning. She had freckles everywhere, and I wanted to kiss every single one. And the sounds she made? Sweet Jesus. When I heard the little catch in her throat, it made my heart speed up every time.

I clung to my control because I was going to make sure she found her release before I did. It might kill me first, but I was determined.

I kept the pace slow and the roll of my hips into hers subtle. The pull and glide of her core nudged me closer and closer to the edge of my control.

I opened my eyes. I had to see her fly apart. I propped myself up on my elbow, adjusting my angle as I reached between us to tease my fingers right at the point of our joining. Her clit was swollen and wet. Her eyes opened wide, and she cried out, her channel clenching hard on my cock.

My own release had been building, so tight inside. I finally let go, drawing out of her once more and doing my damnedest to control my surge inside her. Even then, I knew it was rough. Electricity sizzled at the base of my spine as my balls tightened. Everything spun loose and harsh pleasure thundered through my body.

I shifted my weight to the side, rolling so that Valentina was resting on me. I was fucking laid flat. By her. I felt wrecked and washed ashore as I tried to catch my breath and make sense of what just happened.

I was still inside her and could feel occasional ripples from the aftershocks of her climax. I didn't realize it, but I was idly sifting my fingers through her hair, the silky locks sliding in loops.

After a few moments, I felt her lift her head. Opening my eyes, I found her wide gaze waiting for me. Her cheeks were still flushed, and her lips swollen from our kisses.

That was all it took. Just one look and I wanted her. Again.

I wasn't accustomed to feeling like this. I'd wager I never had. This was different. It stirred deep waters, sliding into the dark corners of my heart that I thought would stay permanently cast in shadow.

At first, Valentina's gaze was contemplative, but a little glint flashed in her eyes. I felt her smile coming before I saw it.

"That was perfect," she said.

I'd admit, I felt damn good. I felt my lips twitching. Instead of fighting it, I gave in with a chuckle, untangling my hand from the ends of her hair and tucking several curls behind her ear.

She startled me by pressing on her hands and rising up. Sweet hell. Valentina sitting astride me just might kill me. Her rosy pink nipples and those freckles—oh my God, those freckles. I loved every single one.

"Easy," I murmured when she shifted, and I saw the slightest bit of a hint of pain pass across her features.

Valentina twisted her lips and cocked her head to the side. "You're bossy."

I laughed. I couldn't remember the last time I laughed with a woman like that. Maybe not ever.

Chapter Twenty-One

LUCAS

Rain struck my cheeks, coming down fast and hard. Thunder rumbled in the distance, and the sky lit up with a bolt of lightning, bright enough to illuminate the mountain ridge nearby.

"You got that?" I called over to Dawson.

"Got it," he replied, his words barely audible through the downpour.

The storm had rolled in late this afternoon. Slashing winds brought a tree down across the highway and into the path of a car. Dawson and I were both on duty for the crew this weekend. We'd driven out to the accident scene together to rendezvous with the EMT team and the police.

By some miracle, the three passengers in the car didn't appear injured; however, they were definitely trapped. Our chief had called ahead to get the power cut here because on its way down, the tree had knocked out two power lines.

I was frankly surprised the power hadn't gone out on its own. From the looks of the sky earlier, I'd known this storm was going to be bad. It wasn't even dark yet, but it might as well have been.

Dawson and I were tasked with getting this tree off the vehicle and out of the way. We were using a series of ropes with an assist from a man who lived nearby and had stopped with his chainsaw. Dawson deftly tied the rope I had tossed over around one of the massive limbs before he stepped back and gave it a good yank.

We worked in the heavy rain with thunder and lightning rumbling around us for a solid hour. When all was said and done, the parents and their young son were more scared than anything else. The tree had fallen across the front of the car, cracking the side of the windshield and crushing part of the roof, but otherwise, it missed them entirely.

Dawson and I drove back to Stolen Hearts Lodge a while later, drenched and tired. He took off to his cabin because he stayed here full-time, unlike me. He didn't waste much time before he gave me a wave and jogged into the trees.

I stood in the rain with my bag over my shoulder for a moment, undecided. I was technically staying in a small room in the offices above the vet clinic. It was perfectly comfortable. Jackson had it set up for when he needed to monitor animals after surgery. Comfort aside, I didn't want to go there.

I wanted to go straight to Valentina, but I didn't know if she would be in her cabin yet, and I didn't know if that was pushing things too far, too fast. Before I consciously made my decision, my feet made it for me, turning in the rain and striding toward Valentina's cabin. With darkness falling, I didn't expect anyone to notice me out here. Conveniently, for my sake, Dawson's cabin was in a different direction.

A few minutes later, I lifted my head, looking through the blur of the rain to see the light on the porch of her cabin beckoning me. I couldn't tell just yet if she was here. I knew from last night she left a light on inside.

Jogging the remaining distance, I stepped onto the porch and gave my head a shake. After a quick knock and no answer, I let out a sigh, brushing away a drop of rain rolling down my cheek.

The last time I felt comfortable just walking into some woman's place when she wasn't there was back when I was dating Melissa in college. Even though I'd gone on to marry Melissa and we had Rylie, I could safely say I hadn't felt the kind of intensity for her that Valentina elicited.

Simply contemplating that reality almost sent me running, yet the force of my draw to Valentina was too damn powerful. I couldn't seem to make my feet move and do the practical thing, the not-fucking-crazy thing and walk back to the vet clinic to stay there.

Just as I was considering what to do, I heard my name. With the sound of rain drumming on the roof above, I could hardly hear. Looking through the trees, I saw Valentina approaching through the rain. It was the hottest part of summer, yet the rain was still cool. Valentina didn't even have a jacket on.

Her T-shirt was plastered to her, and her curls were flat. It wasn't too far of a walk from the lodge to here, but it was a true downpour. Lightning cracked, lighting up the sky and illuminating her.

An unfamiliar sense of protectiveness hit me like a bolt, crackling like lightning. Before I knew it, I dropped my bag and stepped off the porch, running to meet her. I didn't like that she was soaked, not with the lightning and the thunder vibrating around us in this hell of a storm.

Just as the sky lit up again, I reached her. And she smiled. My heart felt as if a ray of sun was shining on it.

"What are you doing?" I asked as I basically dragged her back with me onto the porch.

Out of the rain, Valentina brushed her hand across her forehead and looked up at me through her eyelashes. "Walking home," she said, stating the quite obvious fact. "What are you doing?"

"Coming to see you."

My eyes, because they were greedy, dipped down to see her nipples pressing against her wet T-shirt, and I suddenly wondered who else had seen her.

Dude, what the hell?

That was my skeptical mind, my cynical mind. Because it made absolutely no fucking sense for me to be wondering who had seen Valentina like this. Logically, she left the lodge perfectly dry and got wet on her walk home. Given the rain, no one was hanging around to ogle anyone. Except perhaps me.

It was just that I didn't want anybody else to be aware of how perfect her breasts were, particularly when outlined by drenched cotton.

"Come on," she murmured, slipping her hand through my elbow and giving me a little tug. Snagging my bag, I let her lead me into her cabin.

If she had any thoughts about me unexpectedly showing up, she didn't share them. We stepped inside, and I looked over at her. She was shivering. The cool air conditioning inside was chilly.

Rubbing her hands up and down her arms, she strode toward the bathroom, peeling her clothes off on the way. Dropping my bag by the bed, I wasn't even thinking when I found myself following her. I paused long enough to kick off my boots and hang my raincoat by the door. Wordlessly, I stepped into the bathroom to find her naked and leaning into the shower to turn it on.

I was hard instantly. I wanted her.

So. Damn. Fiercely.

She was unlike any woman I'd ever known. Her refreshing openness, her comfort with herself just how she was.

"You need a shower too," she observed, stepping close to me.

I dipped my head because there was a freckle I wanted

to kiss on her shoulder. My lips traveled, finding that sweet spot in the little dip above her collarbone.

She let out a soft sound in the back of her throat, and it electrified me. Although I could see the wild flutter of her pulse in her neck, she was all business, swiftly unbuttoning my jeans as steam began to fill the room. I nudged my chin toward the shower because it was clear she was still cold with her skin covered in goose bumps.

"Get in the shower. I'll be right behind you."

That was how I found myself in the shower with sexy, sweet Valentina. With bubbles rolling over her skin and steam billowing around us, I couldn't help myself. The moment we started kissing, I was done for.

With the feel of her luscious curves pressed against me, all slick and soapy, it was an act of pure discipline to keep from fucking her hard against the tile wall. All made worse by the fact she threw herself into it. Kissing Valentina was like getting caught in a wave, dragged straight into the riptide of desire.

She wasn't shy, not even a little, as her hands mapped my body, squeezing my ass and nearly pushing me over the edge when she curled her palm around my cock and stroked up and down. Scrambling for control, I spun us to the side, pressing her back against the tile. Bending low, I sucked a nipple in my mouth, teasing the other between my thumb and forefinger.

Every little sound she made was a light lash of the whip cracking at the lust driving me. Still toying with her nipples, I slipped my fingers through her damp curls, finding the core of her hot and slick with arousal. Mindful she might be sore, I teased my fingers through her folds lightly before sliding one finger inside. I heard the sound of her head falling against the tile behind her and lifted her knee, hooking it over my shoulder as I knelt and brought my mouth to her.

I breathed in the salty, musky scent of her, slowly licking over the opening of her swollen pink folds. With the hot water falling down around us, I added another finger to the first. Settling in, I nearly made myself crazy by bringing her to the edge again and again with my mouth and fingers.

"Lucas," she gasped, tugging at my hair.

I paused, glancing up. Her skin was flushed all over from the heat of the shower. Her red hair was wet and dark, falling down around her shoulders as the water ran over her. I ached, so swollen with need for her. But that was not how I'd find my release tonight.

"Oh my God, don't stop!" she muttered, her hips rocking forward.

I didn't need to be told what to do, but I loved having her do it. I returned to my task of devouring her. Another swirl of my tongue around her clit with my fingers buried deeply in her core, and I felt it when she snapped, her entire body going taut as she cried out my name.

I drew away slowly and stood. When she opened her eyes, I kissed her. Because I couldn't stop myself.

She sighed into our kiss, her hand sliding up my chest and curling around my neck. Before I knew it, she had my cock in her hands and was shimmying down. I opened my mouth to say something, to make sure she knew this wasn't about returning the favor, but then I looked down. Through the curtain of water, I saw her blue eyes bright and her mouth curling in a slight smile, and I couldn't form a single word.

Chapter Twenty-Two

VALENTINA

With my own climax still sending little aftershocks of pleasure through me, I swirled my tongue around the tip of Lucas's cock. I wasn't about to let him stop me tonight.

Beyond photographs—and trust me, there were plenty to be found online—his was the only cock I'd seen in the flesh. It was glorious — long, thick, and hard, the skin velvety under my touch. There was a hint of salt to the taste of him. I heard the low groan from his throat and smiled as I settled in to explore every inch of him.

He pulsed under my touch as I spun my tongue around the head and then drew him into my mouth, taking him in as far as I could until the thick crown bumped the back of my throat. His hand tangled in my wet hair. I had no idea what I was doing, but it didn't seem to matter. It seemed quite simple—lick, suck, stroke. Over and over again.

With Lucas gasping my name on a low growl, I kept at it. His hand gripped my hair tightly, and the sting on my scalp felt good. I savored every moment of this. I intended to wring every drop out of the experience I could.

I guessed I would only get so many opportunities like

this with him because he seemed conflicted about us. It was good I didn't expect anything from him.

When I took him in deeply again, sliding my fist down as I tested the weight of his balls in my hand, I felt his entire body tighten. He murmured something, drawing my gaze up just as he pulled back swiftly, fisting his cock. His release spilled onto my breasts, washing off immediately with the water still raining down around us.

I straightened, feeling my smile stretch across my face. Lucas's head had fallen back against the tile, but his eyes were still on me. He shook his head slowly, a grin tugging at the corners of his mouth.

"Jesus, Valentina," he murmured as he lifted a hand. He was almost lazy in his motion, sliding it up to cup the back of my head as he brought my lips to his again.

The kiss was brief but hot. I loved the feel of him. Even when he relaxed, his body was all hardened muscle. I belatedly realized what my father would've had to say about Lucas's comment and giggled.

Lucas reached around me, lathering his hands with the soap. Then his touch was sliding over me, soaping me all over.

"What's so funny?" he asked.

"I was just thinking what my father would say when you used the Lord's name in vain. I don't even care." Another giggle escaped.

Lucas's eyes widened slightly, and he laughed, throwing his head back. I wiped my hands in the soap on my body and returned the favor, smearing the bubbles on him.

"What's so funny?" I repeated his question.

"Darlin', I'm laughing at the same thing as you. If you wanted a man who didn't use the Lord's name in vain, I am *not* that man."

"Good thing that's not the kind of man I want," I murmured.

His gaze sobered. "Please, please don't tell me you were searching out some wild guy to show you the dark side."

"No." I nudged him with my elbow. "It's not like that, it's just ..." I paused, letting out a little sigh. "I love my parents, and they mean well, but sometimes, it's all a bit much. I don't really think God cares if people swear."

Something flickered in his gaze, and he nodded slowly. "I agree on that point."

I didn't know what happened at that moment, but Lucas pulled back slightly. Not in the physical sense, but I could feel him practically slamming down shields around himself.

I did what I always did when I wasn't sure about something. I just carried on and kept my thoughts to myself. I wanted to ask him questions, but while I might not be an expert at relationships, I knew when the timing wasn't right.

———

Days later, I leaned my elbows on the table, glancing at Evie and Grace. Sitting across from me, Dani caught my eyes, rolling her eyes so hard I wouldn't have been surprised if they fell out. We were at Wake & Bake, a local café in downtown Stolen Hearts Valley.

With a sigh, she glanced back and forth between Evie and Grace. "I can't believe y'all are still upset with each other."

Evie crossed her arms and cast a glare at Grace. "Well, she's just being ridiculous. It was a joke."

"I feel like I'm missing something here," I interjected as I paused to take a sip of my coffee.

Dani sighed again. "Here's the short history. They've been friends forever. Evie gave Grace some grief about her high school boyfriend moving back to town. Grace didn't appreciate it. The end."

Grace cast her eyes to Evie. "I might've overreacted."

Evie twisted her bracelet. "And he's been gone for so long

that I forgot it was a sore subject. I shouldn't have teased you about him."

When I glanced at Grace, I saw the pain reflected in her eyes and sensed that perhaps whomever this man was, he meant quite a bit to her. I wasn't about to share my observation right now, though. It certainly didn't seem to be the time.

Grace took a big breath and nodded. "Well, it's not like I talk about it."

"Oh, don't worry, I won't forget because I hate when you don't talk to me. I mean, it's only been a day or so, but ..." Evie said with a slow grin.

Grace rolled her eyes. "Ditto. Does this mean I can ask you to do my hair?"

I'd learned Evie was a rocking hairdresser on the side. Evie's eyes lit up. "Oh, yes! Can we use the staff kitchen? I want to practice the rainbow colors if you'll let me."

Grace's smile was wide. "Of course!"

Their eyes swung to Dani. Before they could even ask anything, she answered, "Of course. The hair dye has to stay in the utility sink, though. Nowhere near the restaurant kitchen. Are we clear?"

"Abso-freaking-lutely," Evie replied with a vigorous nod.

Dani glanced at them with a smile as the owner, Nancy Hill, arrived to check on us. "How're y'all doing over here?"

"I could use a little more coffee," I replied, lifting my mug.

Of course, she had a coffeepot in her hand and promptly topped off every coffee mug on the table. After we ordered a variety basket of bakery goods, Nancy hurried off. Wake & Bake Café was a cute little place, apparently named back when Nancy and her husband, Dan, enjoyed smoking pot when they were younger and thought the name was the perfect pun for a café.

I loved coming here with the girls from the lodge, and we tried to make the trip about once a week or so. The café was in the middle of downtown. Stolen Hearts Valley had a cute little main street with a mix of old and new buildings. The café was housed in an old Colonial home, a small square house with a bright blue roof. Wide plank hardwood flooring, soft cream-colored walls, and tall windows created an inviting, open space. Small round tables were scattered in the front with a counter for ordering at the back.

After Nancy delivered our bakery goodies, our conversation returned to Grace's hair.

"So you're really okay with me trying the rainbow colors?" Evie asked, her eyes bright.

"Yup. I want it to be subtle, though, like it's just shimmering in the light."

"I am *all* over this." Evie popped a small muffin in her mouth and grinned.

"I think we should make it an event," Dani added.

"An event?" I queried.

Dani grinned. "We make it a girls' night, hang out in the back together, and have wine."

I lifted one of my curls, eyeing the color. Before I could even voice my contemplation aloud, Evie chimed in, "Don't even think about it. Your color is incredible, and your curls are amazing. Normally, I am all over figuring out something fun, but I can't do anything that will top your natural state. I guess you could shorten it, but even that seems like a shame. Your hair is glorious."

She reached over from where she sat at an angle across from me, catching the end of one of my curls. Pulling it all the way out, she grinned as it bounced back against my shoulder when she released it. "Amazing."

I spun a curl around my fingers. "But it might be fun to try something different."

Dani shook her head. "Don't. Evie's right; your hair is amazing."

"I guess if you were bored, you could straighten it for the fun of it. But only something temporary," Grace suggested.

I sipped my coffee. "Fine. I actually like my hair, but it'll be fun to see how yours turns out and have a girls' night."

"You don't have to be the one getting your hair done for that," Dani said, nudging me with her shoulder. "Any time the rest of us go under Evie's scissors or coloring magic, you'll be there for all the fun."

I took a breath, letting it out slowly. "I'm so glad I got this job."

"We are too," Dani replied swiftly as Evie and Grace nodded in agreement.

Nancy passed by, quickly filling our mugs and carrying on. At that moment, the door to the café opened with Jackson stepping through, immediately followed by Lucas.

The moment my eyes landed on Lucas, heat bloomed from my core and radiated outward. Almost as if he knew I was there, Lucas's gaze cast across the room, coming to a stop when he saw me. I'd read my share of romance novels, and one of those *moments* happened.

For several beats, it felt as if we were alone, the murmur of voices around us falling away. Although he was a good twenty feet away, I could feel the heat of his gaze from across the room, a sizzle shimmering through the air between us. His gaze dropped from mine when Jackson said something to him.

When I brought my attention back to the table, I found three pairs of extremely curious eyes waiting for me. I knew my cheeks were probably red enough to match my hair, so I quickly stuffed one of the tiny muffins in my mouth, chewing rapidly to give myself something to do.

"Wow, that was a *look*," Evie observed, unabashedly looking from me to over at Lucas. I was relieved he and Jackson had stepped up to the counter and were ordering.

"It sure was," Grace added. "Is there something going on with you and Lucas?"

Seeing as Dani knew a little bit, but certainly not *all* of it,

I figured there was no sense in lying. I lifted one of my shoulders in a shrug, striving to be casual. "Maybe."

"Maybe?" Evie leaned forward on her elbows. "This is huge."

"Why is it huge?" I asked.

Grace arched a brow, pursing her lips slightly. "Lucas doesn't get involved with anyone. I don't know if it's personal, but ever since everything went down ..." she began before looking at Dani.

"She knows," Dani chimed in, answering Grace's unspoken question. "They're about to walk over here, so let's not make it a thing."

Evie leaned back in her chair, nodding solemnly. "Of course not."

"All right, when are we doing the hair dye thing because we are getting the scoop on this?" Grace asked.

"Tomorrow," Evie said just as Jackson and Lucas turned away from the counter with coffee cups in their hands and walked in our direction.

I had no idea how to handle these situations. I didn't know what to call what was happening with Lucas and me because I'd never navigated the waters of casual social interactions when it involved a man who knew me intimately.

It didn't help that my pulse had gone haywire and butterflies were spinning in circles in my belly. It also didn't help that I could hardly breathe. You'd think breathing would be something I could handle. I shouldn't have to think about it.

I hoped they were only coming over to say hello, but that hope clashed with the wish that Lucas would walk over and kiss me and maybe even declare to the world he loved me. That was how out of my element I was. I was having fantasies about love when we barely talked about anything.

It had been several days since our last night together over the weekend. There had been the shower night and another night when he sent me flying more than once. I wondered how I had survived without sex this far in my life. He had even sweet-talked me into trying out my pink vibrator with him.

Just thinking about it now made me blush. I didn't know if I could blush any harder at this rate. Even my toenails were probably flushed. I took a fortifying sip of my coffee, catching one of my curls in my fingers and twirling it.

The couple sitting at the table beside us happened to get up just as Jackson and Lucas arrived. "Hey there, mind if we grab your table?" Jackson asked.

"Of course not, we're leaving," the man said.

Jackson and Lucas sat down, mere feet away from us. It so happened that Lucas was seated opposite me. Although I told myself not to look directly at him, of course my eyes went right there. Because I couldn't help it. It had only been days since the weekend had ended, but I missed him, and it didn't make any sense.

"Well, hey boys," Dani said, immediately starting the conversation.

Lucas's eyes collided with mine again, lingering briefly, the heat in his gaze nearly taking my breath away.

"Hey in return," Jackson replied. "Was wondering where you were."

Dani cocked her head to the side. "I do occasionally leave the restaurant, you know."

Lucas glanced at her, his lips kicking up in a slight smile. "Shocking."

Jackson grinned. "We're headed to a meeting at the station and stopped for coffee on the way. Mind if I snag one of those?" he asked, gesturing to the basket of muffins.

"Of course not," Evie replied, sliding the basket to the edge of the table.

Jackson and Lucas helped themselves, and the conversation carried on around me. I was finding it quite difficult to have Lucas this close and be surrounded by friends, basically forcing me to be socially appropriate. Although I didn't know what I would've done if we'd been alone.

With a mental shake, I sipped my coffee and managed to articulate polite responses during the conversation. Jackson and Lucas stood after a few moments, saying their goodbyes. I felt silly because I wanted to get up and follow Lucas right now and ask him when I could see him again. But that was the thing. He had other priorities, and they didn't always include nights with me.

I managed what I thought to be a socially appropriate goodbye to both of them, watching as they walked out. Just as Lucas reached the door, he glanced back, and it felt as if a flame licked through the air between us. With just a look, he had me hot and bothered all over again.

After the door closed behind him, I almost choked on my next sip of coffee when Evie turned to me, her brows hitching up. "Whoa. Something is totally going on."

Dani narrowed her eyes. "If Lucas has the hots for her, so be it."

In a funny way, I almost wanted to let this keep rolling, if only because I could use the collective wisdom of about a thousand women at this point.

I caught Dani's eye. "I don't mind."

"You sure? Because you *will* hear more about this than you ever wanted."

My cheeks were still hot from that searing look from Lucas. I shrugged again. "So what? Here's the thing, we kissed and maybe more."

Dani's eyes widened. "I think I missed half the story."

Meanwhile, Grace and Evie leaned forward together, waiting for me to fill in the blanks. As much as I wanted advice, I wasn't going to tell them everything. Somehow, it felt too private, too intimate. I felt protective of Lucas and had no idea what to do with that.

Chapter Twenty-Three

LUCAS

That evening I sat on the couch, watching Rylie carefully assemble a puzzle. Her dark hair was pulled up in a ponytail held in place with a bright pink elastic. She was a combination of feminine and tomboy and had been ever since she had a preference. Pink was her absolute favorite color, and she loved overalls and trucks. Today, she was wearing a modified pair of overalls cut into shorts with a tank top underneath. They hung loosely over her thin frame. It didn't seem to matter how much she ate, she stayed skinny. I'd even asked her doctor about it at her checkup last month, but she had assured me Rylie was just fine.

"Daddy, this one?" she asked, holding up a piece.

I leaned forward, eyeing the puzzle. The piece she held was white with a dash of red. Jade sat on the floor on the other side of the coffee table and snorted slightly. "Good luck with that one. I tried to find its spot too."

Scanning the puzzle, I narrowed down an area and pointed, watching as Rylie studied it carefully for another moment before gleefully fitting the piece into a section.

I flicked my eyes up to the clock. "About time for dinner. You ready?" I asked.

Rylie looked up, her ponytail bouncing when she nodded. "Yes! What are we having?"

I slid my gaze to Jade who replied, "Your favorite potato casserole, sweet pea. Come on." She stood, holding her hand out for Rylie as I pushed up from the couch and walked toward the kitchen.

"Wash your hands first," I called as Rylie broke free and started to run to the small round table beside the kitchen. She immediately changed course, veering down the hallway in the back.

"You staying?" I asked as Jade reached my side and leaned against the end of the island.

"Not tonight. I promised I'd cover a shift at Lost Deer Bar."

"Please don't tell me you need the money because I'll insist on paying you more if you do." The oven timer buzzed right then, and I turned away.

"I don't need the money. I'm just doing a favor." Rylie returned from the bathroom, wiping her hands on her overalls. "Gotta go," Jade said as she knelt and held her arms out.

Rylie skidded to a stop, swinging her arms around Jade's neck and planting a noisy kiss on her cheek. "Good night, JJ."

Jade straightened before casting a quick wink and a wave my way as she hooked her purse over her arm.

Some nights, it was damn tempting to sit on the couch and watch television when Rylie and I had dinner, but I didn't want that to be the only way we spent time together. We were about halfway through dinner when my emergency cell phone buzzed.

Rylie knew what that meant. "You have to go, Daddy. Should I go with you?" she asked.

I kept my "oh fuck" silent as I looked over at her. I wasn't even thinking when Jade left. Not that I'd have asked her to stay, but I was on duty tonight. I needed to call my mom and see if she could come over. "I'll figure it out, sweet pea," I replied, standing from the table and striding into the living room.

After calling in to confirm I'd be there as soon as I could, I quickly texted my mother only to get her reply that she was still running errands in Asheville and wouldn't be able to make it back for an hour and a half. When we were backup on call, blessedly, part of the team was always on duty full-time, so we had some leeway to get there. That leeway didn't extend to an hour and a half, though.

My next option would be Shay, Dani, or... My thoughts trailed off. My last option was Valentina. Before I even thought about it, I pulled up her number, and my thumbs were texting her. I couldn't even admit I wanted her to come over. Because that meant a chance for me to see her.

I reasoned she clearly had experience with babysitting. All she would need to do tonight was the bedtime routine.

Me: Hey, it's Lucas. I'm in a bit of a bind and could use a favor. I got a call out for the emergency team, and my usual babysitting sources are unavailable. Rylie loved when you helped out with Shay, so I was wondering if you might have a few hours tonight.

I hit send so fast I immediately wondered if I'd lost my mind. Though if I was being honest with myself, I'd lost my damn mind over Valentina weeks ago. Having her come to my house to babysit was another level of crazy.

I ran a hand through my hair, glancing at Rylie who was still steadily eating. She was a slow eater. Most of the time, I didn't mind, but I'd had to teach myself patience for that. I tended to shovel food in my mouth. That was what happened when your life was a flat-out run just to keep up.

My phone buzzed in my palm, and I glanced down.

Valentina: Of course. Should I come to you?

My heart felt as if it were tumbling in my chest. Out of the blue, or so it seemed, my throat tightened with emotion. Of course Valentina would say yes. She was that kind of person. I doubted it would ever occur to her to say no. I was overjoyed at nothing more than her agreeing to babysit. My out-of-proportion response wasn't something I could contemplate now.

Lifting my phone again, I tapped out my reply.

Me: Yes. If you don't mind. I'm not sure what time I'll be back. This way, Rylie can fall asleep here.

Valentina: OK, what's your address?

Once again, my thumbs were ahead of the rest of me. I typed it out in a hot second with her reply coming just as quickly.

Valentina: Be there in about 15 minutes.

My mind was jangling with a mix of thoughts and emotions. I was fucking insane. But in the end, I needed someone to watch Rylie or to scrounge someone up to cover for me. My options at this hour were limited for both.

Dawson was often good in a pinch, but I knew he was probably already well into several beers at Lost Deer Bar. I returned to the table, slipping into the chair beside Rylie. She glanced up. "So what's happening?" Happening was a new favorite word for her, a rather big word.

"Do you remember Valentina? The lady who was with Shay last week when I dropped you off?"

Rylie's smile split wide. "Valentine. That's her name, Daddy. You're saying it wrong."

I didn't have the heart to correct her. Not that it mattered. I sincerely doubted Valentina would care one way or the other if Rylie called her Valentine.

"Well, she's on her way over. She'll stay to help you get ready for bed. You'll probably be asleep when I get home. Do me a favor and finish up, okay?" I asked, nodding toward the few bites of potato casserole left on her plate.

Rylie carefully took her remaining bites, her feet drumming on the legs of her chair. I didn't give myself much credit for it, what with my mom and my sister spending as much time with Rylie as me, but I was beyond relieved she was a social girl. She loved new people and tended to easily adjust as long as she was comfortable.

Not that I had many parents to talk with, but I'd heard my share of stories about screaming tantrums and refusals to go to bed and so on and so forth when babysitters were needed. Rylie had her moments, but they were rare. Her pediatrician had even commented on her laid-back temperament.

Despite my tangled feelings about Melissa, it still hurt she wasn't here to see her little girl. Somehow, I doubted we would be together if she were, but she had a special daughter.

I shoveled the rest of my dinner in and stood to rinse our plates. Rylie hurried to her bedroom to pull out her favorite stuffed bear along with her two current favorite bedtime stories. When she returned to the living room, her ponytail even more lopsided now, there was a knock on the front door.

"I got it!" Rylie announced as she promptly dropped the bear and the books on the floor.

I turned, about to tell her to pick everything up, but then reconsidered. Not now.

Standing on her tiptoes, she turned the doorknob with both hands. I forced myself to wait in the kitchen because I knew the moment I saw Valentina, I would want to kiss her. Just like I did every time I saw her now. I needed to keep some distance between us to curb the temptation.

The door opened slowly without much momentum since Rylie was only so strong. A blast of humidity came in from outside. Valentina stood in the doorway, her hair more curly than usual, likely due to the lingering heat from the day.

"Hi, Valentine," Rylie said, sweeping one of her hands in a wide arc.

"Hey, Rylie," Valentina replied with a smile, kneeling to greet her.

Rylie's smile went from ear to ear. As Valentina straightened, her eyes caught mine. I hadn't quite adjusted to it, but I was learning that any time I saw Valentina, it was as if lightning jolted me, the air becoming heavy with a sizzle of electricity following.

I rounded the counter, still holding the dishtowel in my hands. "Thanks for coming over on such short notice," I said as I stopped beside Rylie.

Rylie wasn't paying the least bit of attention. She had already turned to gather up her stuffed bear and her two books, carting them over to the couch.

"No problem. Is there anything I should know before you go?" Valentina asked. Her eyes met mine briefly before bouncing away and sliding over to Rylie.

"Not much. She just had dinner. She's got her bedtime routine down." Setting the dishtowel on the counter, I walked over to the couch. Resting my hips onto the edge of it, I glanced at Rylie. "Why don't you tell Valentina your bedtime routine?"

"Valentine," Rylie corrected me.

I caught the twitch of Valentina's lips, but she stayed quiet. I was far too aware of what she was wearing. It was entirely unremarkable. She had on a pair of stretchy leggings that fell to just below her knees, and cowboy boots paired with a gray T-shirt. Even though the fabric was loose, her breasts stretched across the front. I swallowed and looked away. I did *not* need to be lusting after my daughter's short-notice babysitter.

Valentina tucked an errant curl behind her ear and sat down in a chair to one side of the couch. "Please tell me what your schedule is so we get it right."

Rylie's small fingers fiddled with the bear's ear. "I need to brush my teeth and then after that, I wash my hands and change into my jammies. Then I get a bedtime story. Whoever's here reads me the bedtime story, so that's you tonight."

Valentina grinned. "It sounds like you have it all lined out. What time do you usually brush your teeth?"

Rylie reached for my hand, turning it so she could look at the watch on my wrist. "Seven thirty."

"All right. We have a schedule. I think I can handle that, and I'm guessing your dad needs to go."

Rylie leaned over, burrowing her head into my shoulder. As she wrapped her arms around my waist, I held her close. "I do. You be a good girl, okay?"

Leaning away, she nodded, watching as I stood. Valentina stood with me.

"Is there anything else I need to know?" she asked as I strode toward the door where my go-bag was always waiting.

"Nah. That's pretty much it. Bedtime usually isn't an issue for her, so it should be fine." I snagged my keys and slung my bag on my shoulder, glancing down at her. The urge to kiss her was almost overpowering, but we had an audience —a specific, very curious audience of one. "I'm not sure what time I'll be back. As soon as I have an ETA, I'll text."

"I'll stay as long as you need me." At the last minute, she reached out, catching my hand and giving it a quick squeeze. "Be safe."

My heart tumbled again, and I wanted to pull her close. I didn't go through life thinking much about how alone I was, but it was a bald fact. Oh, I had Rylie, my mother, my father, and my sister, but I didn't have a partner. Back when I thought Melissa and I meant something, I savored that knowledge.

Swallowing through the thickness in my throat, I nodded. "Always."

I needed to go, and I needed to get the hell out of this moment before I did something stupid.

———

Hours later, after helping a pair of idiots who decided to try to rock climb in the dark and got stranded high on a ledge, along with Jackson and Wade, I headed back home. I belatedly realized I needed to let Valentina know I was on my way. Pulling off the side of the road, I quickly texted her and then kept driving.

It was still hot out, but I had the windows open. That was something I loved. After darkness fell, the air was rich with the lingering scents of flowers and greenery as it cooled. The moon was high above the Blue Ridge Mountains, shining in the inky blue night sky with stars scattered amidst the drifting clouds.

Anticipation was humming in my body. I had taken things too far with Valentina, and I didn't know how the hell to back out. I wouldn't lie. I wanted her something fierce. Something about her authenticity struck a chord in me, the vibration echoing through my body. I never thought I would want more with a woman. After losing Melissa when she died, it had been hard to think about letting someone matter that much. Life seemed too fickle.

I recalled the doctor explaining to me that it was possible Melissa had a weakness in that artery in her brain her entire life. In hindsight, I believed the doctor meant for that to comfort me. Instead, it only hammered home the point that life was fucking random.

All I wanted to do was shelter Rylie from the world. So there was that, and then the rest of the fucking train wreck when I found out about Melissa's affair. Talk about having your feet knocked out from under you when it came to romance.

So, yeah, I hadn't planned on this. I hadn't even considered I could be susceptible. But then Valentina was one of a kind. I loved that she sometimes slapped her hand over her mouth whenever a swear word slipped out, but she didn't really care. It was just habit. By some fucking miracle, she had stayed a virgin until me.

There I was, driving home on a warm, humid night in the

mountains, and a woman I was coming to think of as mine was waiting there for me. Not once did it cross my mind to worry about Rylie tonight. Valentina was just that trustworthy.

I turned down my drive, dimming the lights and slowing as I passed through the trees. After I stepped out of my truck, I leaned my head back to look at the sky. An owl called in the darkness, another answering. Crickets chirped, and cicadas hummed. I took a deep breath, steeling myself to keep myself in check when I went inside.

I didn't have a map for this. Not at all.

Valentina hadn't replied to my text. I let myself in quietly, immediately arrested by the sight of her sound asleep on the couch.

My heart started up, thrashing in my chest. It shouldn't mean that much to see her asleep in my house, but it did. She was on her side, a throw pillow tucked under her head with one arm resting on her belly and the other curled under the pillow. Her hair obscured half of her face, and her knees were drawn up.

She'd kicked off her cowboy boots and wore a pair of bright pink socks. I smiled, wondering if Rylie had seen those. She would've been thrilled with her love of all things pink. I slipped out of my shoes and set my bag down quietly.

I walked stealthily down the short hallway, glancing into Rylie's bedroom. Her nightlight was on, and she was sound asleep. I leaned over her bed and pressed a kiss to her forehead, adjusting the sheets over her shoulders. She didn't even budge. Tiptoeing out of her room, I left her door cracked open.

Returning to the living room and approaching the couch, I almost thought Valentina was a mirage and would go up in smoke.

She wasn't. Her breathing was even and steady, and she didn't even stir. I didn't know if she preferred to leave, so I needed to check.

"Valentina?" I whispered.

She murmured something in her sleep. I glanced at my watch. It was going on one in the morning. I had no idea what her schedule was today, but I knew I'd be up by five thirty a.m.

Whether it was rational or not, I somehow persuaded myself it was best if she slept in a bed. I didn't listen to the voice reminding me she'd be perfectly fine out here on the couch. I bundled her into my arms, telling myself if she woke, then I'd ask if she wanted to leave or sleep on the couch.

She didn't. I carried her into my bedroom because that was the only other bed in the house beside Rylie's.

Valentina wasn't heavy, but she was warm, soft, and lush in my arms. She stirred briefly and then burrowed her head into my shoulder with a sigh. With my heart thudding, I nudged my bedroom door open with an elbow and carried her in, closing it behind me. I eased her onto the bed, pulling the covers over her, thinking any minute she was going to wake up. She didn't.

I took a record fast shower to wash off the grime of the day. When I returned to the bedroom, I thought for sure she would have woken, but she hadn't. I tried to tell myself I just wanted her to get a good night's sleep.

The truth was, I didn't want her to leave.

I could've tried to tell myself it had something to do with thinking I could be slick and catch a stolen quickie with her. Not that she was a quickie kind a girl, or that I was a quickie kind a guy, but I couldn't even make that argument. Don't get me wrong, if the opportunity presented itself, it would absolutely happen. But what I wanted was to sleep with her beside me.

When I slipped between the cool sheets, I held my breath, only letting it out when she stirred, rolling against me, her warm curves soft against my side. It still took me a few minutes to fall asleep, if only because I wanted to imprint the feel of this moment in my memory.

I fell asleep to the rhythm of her breath and the silky feel of her skin with her foot tucked between my calves and her hand splayed on my chest. Just above the thump of my heart.

Chapter Twenty-Four

VALENTINA

Daybreak came in fragments—a shaft of sunlight across the bed, my consciousness flickering awake, the feel of a muscled arm curled around my back, the hum of the air conditioner, cotton sheets against my skin, and a warm male body beside me.

My eyes flew open abruptly. Oh. My. I was curled up against Lucas. In his bed.

Before my brain was fully awake, my hand shifted on his chest, exploring the muscled planes and the dusting of hair. Lucas was all man even when he was asleep.

He stirred, his eyes opening. In the muted light of morning, they were bright and sleepy. Rolling his head to the side, he scrubbed a hand through his hair and smiled.

My heart promptly did a few cartwheels. I knew I was getting in over my head, but the way I felt right now was downright treacherous for me. Because I couldn't let myself go there. I felt my lips curling into a smile.

"Mornin'," he murmured, his hand circling lazily on my back. "You were asleep when I got home last night, and I didn't have the heart to wake you up."

Before I had a chance to reply, he glanced toward the clock on the nightstand. I suddenly became aware he was aroused. My eyes were drawn to the distinct shape of his arousal under the sheets.

I wanted—oh, how I wanted—to touch him.

He looked back in my direction. "Unfortunately, I have to get up. Considering that Rylie will be up soon, it's probably best if you get up too."

"Oh, of course." I started to scramble up, but his arm caught me, tugging me right back against his chest, which I didn't mind at all.

"Just a minute," he murmured. His hand slid into my hair, and he pulled me close for a kiss. It was quick, hot, and left me breathless. Nothing more than a brush of his lips against mine, and a sweep of his tongue before he drew back.

I didn't quite know how to interpret the look in his eyes. I watched as he climbed out of bed. He had on fitted briefs that hugged his muscled ass with his arousal clearly visible.

With a glance over his shoulder, he met my gaze. "I gotta be ready in record time so I'm out in the kitchen before Rylie's up. I need a shower to wake me up."

I had no idea how to handle this morning, but I had enough sense to know it was best that Rylie didn't find us in the shower together by accident, so I simply nodded. I was still wearing what I had on last night and figured Lucas must've carried me into the bedroom.

When I heard the water running, I rolled off the bed, my feet landing on the cool hardwood floor. With a deep breath, I gave my head a shake and stood. I straightened my clothes and slipped out of the bedroom. Conveniently, I always kept a little travel toothbrush in my purse. This ranked as the first time I ever actually needed it. I tended to have all kinds of handy things in my purse, including a few Band-Aids, a comb, and hair ties.

Stepping into the bathroom off the living room, I washed my face and quickly brushed my teeth. A side bonus to wild curly hair was it was easy to manage because it was usually messy. I used the comb to tidy it a bit and stepped out of the bathroom to find Lucas already in the kitchen. His hair was damp, and he wore a pair of jeans that hung low on his hips with a T-shirt. My heart thudded in my chest, and I once again wondered what to do. I thought maybe it was best if I left before Rylie woke up.

I stopped beside the rounded edge of the counter just as he turned to face me. His eyes caught mine, and I wished I could climb inside his brain and see what he was thinking. I was unaccountably nervous.

Swallowing, I cleared my throat. "I'm thinking I should get going before Rylie wakes up."

Lucas was quiet for a moment before he shrugged. "Maybe. Although it would be fine if you stayed for breakfast. She might like that." Pausing, he smiled, and my heart practically started cheering. "Actually, she would love it. It's no big thing that you fell asleep on the couch. That's what we'll tell her."

Thump, thump, thump went my heart. He was right, but I still ...

I didn't get to finish that train of thought. I heard a pair of feet coming down the hall, the distinct sound of a small child's half run.

"Valentine!" Rylie called as she rounded the end of the hallway, coming into the living room and veering toward the kitchen.

I turned, squatting down as Rylie made her way over. My heart squeezed. Between my rapidly burgeoning feelings for Lucas and his absolutely precious daughter, my heart was probably going to expire at this rate.

Something was so endearing about a sleepy child. Rylie's dark hair was mussed, and her cheeks were flushed from sleep. She still wore her pajamas.

Her eyes were wide with wonder as she smiled up at me. "You're here! Good morning," she said, swinging her arms around my neck and squeezing tight. I hugged her back, sliding my hand over her hair.

"Good morning. I fell asleep on the couch," I explained, relieved I was actually telling the truth.

The last thing Rylie needed to know was that her father had carried me to bed, and I woke up wanting him so fiercely my body ached with it. Although, I was discovering an almost surefire way to eliminate the desire pounding through my body was the presence of a child. Rylie represented so many reasons why I didn't need to be getting ideas about Lucas.

"JJ does that sometimes. Even Daddy does," Rylie said solemnly.

I ruffled a hand through her hair as I straightened. "I bet."

Rylie was already turning, approaching her father. Lucas leaned down and swung her into his arms, resting her on his hip as he pressed a kiss to her forehead. "Mornin', sweet pea. What'll it be for breakfast?"

Rylie tapped her index finger on the side of her cheek. I bit the inside of my cheeks to keep from laughing because she was too cute.

"Oatmeal with blueberries and brown sugar," she finally announced after appearing to think deeply about it.

"You got it." Lucas's attention was solely on her now. He turned, opening a cabinet that stretched from floor to ceiling and was filled with food. Reaching in, he pulled out a container of oatmeal and a small bag of dried blueberries, which he handed to her.

As Lucas turned, she wiggled.

"Hang on, let me put this down," he said. After setting the oatmeal down, he took the blueberries from her and eased her to the floor.

"Want some breakfast?" she asked.

Like I'd say no. "I'd love some."

After that, it was just a morning. We had breakfast, and

Lucas made a mean cup of coffee. I managed to get my body under control and not let my mind start running down the wild variety of paths I could select. Until it was time to go.

I was covering the late shift for breakfast in the lodge restaurant today. When I stood to leave, there was a knock on the door. Whoever it was didn't even wait, and the door swung open immediately after the knock.

"Morning," a woman called out.

The moment I saw her, I knew she must be related to Lucas. She had the same black hair. It was straight and glossy, pulled up in a ponytail high atop her head. She was slender and probably a good foot shorter than he was. Her green eyes clapped to me immediately.

Of course, I didn't know exactly what she was thinking, but I definitely knew she was assessing me. Rylie immediately ran across the room, calling, "JJ!"

"Hey, Jade," Lucas called over. "Valentina babysat last night in a pinch and fell asleep on the couch."

Seeing as I'd never had a boyfriend, I had zero experience with meeting family. Much less under these circumstances where I didn't know how to define what I was to Lucas. I worried Jade could somehow see right into me and sense my growing feelings for him. Anxiety tightened in my belly, and I swallowed and took a deep breath. I hadn't done anything wrong, but I suddenly felt as if I had.

Jade hugged Rylie to her. "You got me for today. Are you cool with that?"

"Of course!" Rylie wiggled down and swung her arm wildly in my direction. "This is Valentine."

Jade crossed the room toward me, and I actually wiped my hands on my sides, worried she'd feel they were damp.

"Hi," I said, politely holding my hand out.

Jade's palm was cool in mine as she shook my hand, quickly and firmly. "Nice to meet you. I'm sure it was a good thing you could fill in last night."

"Valentine's nice," Rylie said, bumping up against me as she leaned into my hip.

I managed to smile at Jade. "I was glad to help. I met Rylie last week when Lucas brought her out to see if Shay could watch her for a little bit. Shay and I work in the office together at the lodge so ..." My words tapered off, and I shrugged slightly.

I definitely felt as if I were under a microscope—a protective sister microscope. Jade gave me one last careful look, then stepped past me with a nod. Lucas was closing the dishwasher and turned to face us.

At that moment, Rylie piped up, "Can Valentine come over again tonight?"

The adults in the room froze, and I could feel the sudden tension in the air. Lucas, who up to that point had been warm, gave off a cool air. His eyes flicked from Rylie to me and back. "I'm not on call tonight, so I'll be home for dinner."

Jade, wisely in my opinion, immediately created a distraction. "Come on, girl," she said, clapping her hands lightly. "Let's get you out of those pajamas."

She held out her hand as Rylie looked up at me. "Are you staying?"

"I need to get to work. It was sure nice to see you," I said, ruffling her hair and leaning over to press a kiss on the top of her head. I was relieved when Jade called her name again.

I wasn't relieved because of Rylie, but because I wanted to escape the tension. I knew my smile was tight when I looked in Lucas's direction. "Gotta go," I said quickly, not waiting for a response.

I heard Rylie and Jade's voices fading as they walked down the short hallway with Jade keeping up a running commentary of questions. I had already stepped outside and was closing the door when I felt it open again. Turning back, I found Lucas right behind me.

"Thanks again," he said gruffly. "Look, I didn't mean ..."

I didn't give him a chance to finish. "You don't need to worry about what you meant. You're a father, and I get how important it is that nothing be confusing. Don't worry about me."

I sensed he wanted to say more, but now definitely wasn't the time. I may not have known how to read him to well, but I knew what I felt in his reaction when Rylie asked if I could return tonight. That wasn't something he was considering, and that was perfectly okay with me. It had to be.

Chapter Twenty-Five

LUCAS

A few days later, after hearing Rylie ask more times than I cared to count when Valentina would babysit again, I walked into my parents' house for dinner. I'd had a busy day at work with a guided hike and helping Jackson with the new cabins, so I was tired. Jade had texted to let me know she'd bring Rylie over here for dinner. We usually got together like this as a family every few weeks whenever everyone managed to be available.

Rylie's voice carried from the kitchen when I stepped into the living room with the murmur of my mother's more muted reply following. "Hey, sis," I said, toeing my boots off by the door.

Crossing the living room, I sank onto the couch beside Jade where she was knitting. My parents had a simple ranch house. There was a large living room with a fireplace on one side, and a hallway to the back that led to a run of bedrooms. An archway led to the dining room with the kitchen beyond that.

My father ran his own mechanic business in a garage down the street while my mother ran a floral business. In just about every way, I'd had a typical middle-class child-hood. I was lucky. My parents loved each other and me and my sister. I never forgot to count my blessings.

Jade and I hadn't had much time to chat since she met Valentina the other morning, but given our schedules, that wasn't a surprise. We rarely had time to talk for more than a few minutes.

Her green eyes slid sideways, catching mine. Her knitting needles clicked away.

"How's it going?" she asked.

"Same as usual. Just busy. Anything I should know about today with Rylie?"

"Nothing new. She had a small fit when I made her stick to the half hour of TV time. Oh, and she'd like Valentine to come over again."

Jade's slow drawl of Rylie's version of Valentina's name wasn't lost on me. I knew she'd been waiting for a moment to ask about just what the hell Valentina was doing at my house that morning.

I'd had plenty of time to chew on it in my thoughts and decided I might as well tell her the plain truth. In mulling it over, I'd come to a conclusion. It was too damn messy to try to think about bringing a woman into my life with Rylie. I didn't want her to get attached, and there was no way to see into the future.

I might've wanted Valentina—hell, I fucking dreamed about the woman every night—but that didn't mean it was a smart decision to do anything about it.

I met Jade's assessing gaze and rolled my eyes. "Just ask me whatever you want."

"I don't hear a single word about a woman in your life. Then I show up, and it's clear Valentina spent the night there."

Jade actually stopped knitting, which was a sign. She was pissed. Probably not about Valentina specifically, but most likely pissed because I hadn't given her advance notice. I loved my little sister, but we had a kind of reverse situation going on with the protectiveness. That wasn't to say I wasn't protective of my sister, just that Jade was equally so with me. She would kick someone's ass if she thought it was warranted. She'd been downright livid when she found out Melissa had an affair before she died.

Jade's hands fell to her lap, and she idly twirled the end of the yarn around her finger. "It doesn't quite seem as simple as the babysitter falling asleep on the couch."

"She *did* fall asleep on the couch if that's what you're asking." I conveniently left out the fact I'd carried Valentina to my bed.

Jade huffed. "Just tell me what the hell is going on with her."

Leaning my head back, I sighed. "Nothing that night, but more has happened. But I've thought about it since then, and I don't think it's a good idea to let things keep going."

She shook her head sharply. "What the hell, Lucas? First off, if you were thinking about already having someone spend the night, that's too fast for Rylie. But now you're saying nothing happened that night, but it has before?"

I ran a hand through my hair and nodded. "Look, don't give me hell for asking her to babysit. I forgot I was on call that night. Once I got the call out, you were working, and Mom was in Asheville. Valentina did a great job with Rylie when I had to drop her off before with her and Shay, so don't give me shit about that. For the rest, fair enough. You don't need to worry because nothing else is happening."

I rolled my head from side to side, trying to ease the tension bundling there. I had to shy away from thinking about Valentina because I hated cutting things off like this, but it was the only sensible thing to do.

"I'm not telling you not to get involved with her," Jade protested, blowing a puff of air to get a lock of hair out of her eyes.

"Well then, what's your point?" I countered.

"Valentina seems nice."

"Oh, for fuck's sake, Jade. You practically gave her a death stare."

Jade sighed. "Yeah, I thought about it afterward. I didn't mean to come across as bitchy. I'm just ... Well, I guess I'm protective of you."

"You guess?" I replied with a chuckle.

My sister shrugged and cast me a rueful smile.

"I can take care of myself just fine. But I guess it was a good thing. I was about to start letting things go somewhere, and I realized it might not be a smart move. I mean look what's already happened with Rylie. She wants Valentina over all the time. She must ask me about her five times a day."

Jade picked her knitting up again, the rhythmic clicking of the needle starting up. "Rylie loves people. I don't think she's hounding you about Valentina because she somehow notices you have the hots for her. Rylie liking her is no reason not to give her a chance. Your list for that is already too damn long."

"Trying to manage a relationship is too complicated for me. Rylie's doing great, and that's all that matters. Stop worrying about my love life."

"What's a love life?" Rylie asked from the archway.

Oh, dear God. The perils of young children whose ears worked remarkably well.

"We're just talking about friends and stuff, sweet pea," Jade called over.

My mom said something from the kitchen, immediately drawing Rylie away. Jade set her knitting down on the coffee table, uncurling her feet from under her knees. "All I'm saying is stop looking for excuses." At that, she stood and walked into the kitchen.

I followed. Stepping into the kitchen, my eyes scanned the room, finding my dad seated at the table flipping through the newspaper. He still read the actual newspaper every evening. He would put it away when dinner was ready.

"Hey, Dad," I called.

He glanced up with a smile. "Hey, son. Got you some coffee if you need it. I just made it."

Striding over to the counter, I heard Rylie talking to my mother. "Her name is Valentine. She's my new favorite babysitter."

Jade caught my eye as she opened the refrigerator with a sly grin.

Ever tried getting a six-year-old to stop talking about something? Trust me, I'd learned that achievement was near impossible.

My mother's gaze swung to mine. I hadn't said a damn word, but she was too perceptive. She smiled sweetly. "Well, I sure would love to meet her sometime. You know I like to meet everyone who's important to you."

I bit back the curse threatening to slip out and poured my coffee.

———

The following morning, we were at the table while Rylie was selecting bites of her oatmeal that included blueberries when she paused and set her spoon down. "Daddy?"

I finished my sip of coffee, meeting her somber gaze. "Yes?"

"Can Valentine come over soon?"

She looked so damn hopeful. It wasn't that she was more hung up on Valentina than anybody else. She loved making friends, and I loved that about her. My heart squeezed a bit because I was the one deciding Valentina wasn't going to be babysitting again. Every time I tried to push past that wall and convince myself it would be okay to try dating someone, I ran up against the fact that Rylie had already lost her mother. I sure as hell didn't want her to get attached to somebody and then have it not work out. I honestly had no idea how any single parent pulled it off.

Still, I needed to answer carefully. "We don't have any plans for that, sweet pea. But you never know."

Her eyes cast down to her bowl, and she took another bite of oatmeal. The sound of her spoon handle clinking against the bowl was my cue that another question was coming. Her way too curious brain wasn't done with me yet.

"How come you act different around Valentine?"

I had just taken a sip of coffee, and I almost choked on it. Time and again, Rylie showed me just how crazy perceptive she could be. I had always promised myself I would be truthful with her. Yet right now, I didn't have a good answer to her question. In all honesty—despite the voice trying to convince me otherwise, which I was doing my damnedest to ignore—the only truth I knew was that Valentina and I had explosive chemistry. For all I knew, that would fade.

Although, I knew damn well nothing I'd ever felt before came close to the way I felt when I was with Valentina. People often said you'd know love when you felt it. A large part of my heart had an opinion on that matter with Valentina, yet I had no fucking idea how to navigate the landmines created by the uncertainty of the situation.

After another sip of coffee with Rylie's curious gaze steady on me, I set my mug down. "Rylie, Valentina is our friend. I'm not sure if she'll babysit again. You don't have too many babysitters other than grandma and JJ, and for now, it's gonna stay that way. Okay?"

I wasn't answering her question, and I knew it. Rylie's lips tightened slightly, and her forehead furrowed when she squinted. I sensed she knew there was more to the story than that, but at least I could say I hadn't lied. After a moment, she lifted her spoon and scooped up another blueberry. I swore I could feel her disappointment hitting me like an ultrasonic wave.

Rylie didn't ask often, but she occasionally asked if she

would ever have another mother. I had always told her that while her mother wasn't here, she had lots of people who loved her. I knew it to be true, but I also knew it still sucked she lost her mother.

I opened my mouth, thinking I could offer something else to her, but I bit it back, swallowing my words with a sip of coffee.

Chapter Twenty-Six

VALENTINA

A full week had passed since the night I babysat Rylie. Lucas had sent a single text to thank me again, but beyond passing interactions, that was the extent of our communication. Frustratingly, he had largely reverted to the way he used to treat me—glancing looks, brief greetings, and nothing more.

The one exception was the way I felt. Every single time I saw him, my pulse did its usual crazy dance, but that was nothing new. Except now, a flare of hope shot up with my pulse. That was followed with a stinging burn on my heart, which shifted to a throbbing ache in the aftermath of every brief encounter.

Then, there was one day. Hurrying down the hall, I was once again dropping off everyone's mail. It felt like déjà vu when I saw him. Yet again, I came around the corner in the hallway, my hands full of mail and two small boxes. Neither box was addressed to me or him, and whether one of them contained a vibrator was certainly none of my business.

As I was walking too quickly, my shoes skidded a little on the concrete flooring, and I ran into him. This time, I knew it was Lucas before I looked up. I recognized the scent of him and the hard feel of his chest.

The mail went flying. I was flustered, but it was different. My eyes slammed into his, my apology coming out automatically. "I'm sorry!"

He started to lean over, but I shook my head. "Don't worry about it. I've got it."

I gathered up the mail quickly while he ignored me and helped anyway, handing over the small stack of envelopes when I straightened. Adjusting the boxes, I placed the rest of the mail on top of them.

"Thanks," I managed.

He nodded, and there was a flicker in his eyes. It was gone as quickly as it appeared. Clearing his throat, he began, "Valentina, look ..."

Clutching the mail tightly like a shield in front of me, I shook my head sharply. "I have to go."

I wanted this to be a moment when I had some kind of glorious escape, yet that wasn't quite how it felt. Turning away from him, I heard his voice following me, the tug of a string keeping me from walking farther. "Valentina."

My stupid feet turned back in his direction all on their own. I knew my cheeks were red and butterflies were wreaking havoc in my belly. I tried to play it cool while I was anything but cool. Arching a brow, I asked, "Yes?"

"Look, it's not ..."

I didn't let him keep talking. I couldn't handle the pain of it. I could tell by the look on his face he was going to give me some kind of lame explanation, and I didn't need one. Shaking my head sharply, I said, "There's no need to explain this. I completely understand your priorities. Have a nice day."

For just a second, I thought he was going to say something else. His eyes darkened, and he looked pained. I felt that same little tug, even more powerful than when he called my name. This time, I snapped at the invisible tension and turned, practically running down the hallway.

Chapter Twenty-Seven

LUCAS

Standing in that hallway, I watched as Valentina almost ran away from me. My heart was having a fucking tantrum in my chest, and my feet wanted to follow her so badly. That instinct collided with my sense of self-preservation, which tangled up with my protectiveness of Rylie.

No matter how much I wanted Valentina, I sure as hell didn't think she'd signed on for stepping into a parental role. And anyone who got serious with a single parent was doing that whether they wanted to admit it or not. Oh, she was amazing with Rylie. She had a big heart and was so open. I also knew it'd be crazy for me to think she could make promises.

When it came to Rylie, I absolutely could not allow myself to do anything casually. But my heart had more sway than my intellect at this moment. Just as I started to follow Valentina, I heard Dani's voice replying to someone down the hallway. It nudged me out of my insanity.

With dogged determination, I walked in the opposite direction as Valentina.

Chapter Twenty-Eight

VALENTINA

The sun fell across my desk while I tried to work. It was late afternoon, and I hadn't been particularly productive today. All because that stupid encounter with Lucas in the hallway left me feeling shattered. I literally felt as if my heart had tripped and fallen on its face. I hadn't anticipated this. I'd so stupidly thought I could take advantage of the situation.

The few kisses I experienced before Lucas hadn't left me with any lingering feelings. Even though Lucas had a charged effect on my body, I'd thought perhaps I could manage it, and that it was just chemistry. *Silly me.*

I was in a truly, madly, deeply situation.

Shay startled me, popping her head around the corner of my office door. "Coffee break?" she asked, reaching up to adjust the ponytail on her head.

I jumped in my chair, slapping my hand to my chest. "Oh! I didn't even hear you."

"No kidding. That doesn't mean you're gonna say no to a coffee break, though, does it?"

"Definitely not. I could use something to help me focus."

She cocked her head to the side. "Are you okay? You're

the most focused person I know when it comes to numbers. That's why I am so glad we hired you."

Taking a brief deep breath, I contemplated whether to confide in Shay. I wasn't used to having girlfriends, but maybe now was a good time to enjoy the benefits. I could use some advice. "Let's get coffee first."

"On it," she said quickly, spinning out of my doorway.

I heard her feet moving briskly down the hallway and her voice saying hello to the new vet tech Jackson had hired last week. We usually had coffee breaks in my office. For reasons I wasn't entirely clear on, my office had a better view than Shay's. The windows offered a pretty view of the trees and the mountain ridge on the far side of the valley.

With a mental shake, I saved what little I'd managed to do and closed my laptop. I was rounding my desk to sit at the table just as Shay came in with two mugs in her hands. We preferred our coffee the same with just a dash of cream. Shay sat down across from me and slid my coffee cup over. I took a sip, savoring the rich flavor.

"By the way, how come I have the office with a better view? Is it because you want your office closer to Jackson?"

Shay burst out laughing. "My office used to be Jackson and Ash's office. At least, when she was around," she said referring to Jackson's younger sister who wasn't currently in Stolen Hearts Valley. "I kept it because it happened to be the closest one to the clinic offices."

"I think that's sweet."

Shay smiled, her cheeks pinkening slightly. "Things are good right now, but it hasn't always been that way," she offered vaguely.

She didn't discuss it much, but I knew the story. I was so happy she'd found her way to Jackson. Perhaps she could give me some idea of what love was. *Not that it would matter*, I thought morosely.

"Enough about me. What's going on with you?"

I took another sip of my coffee, followed with a deep breath, and replied, "It's Lucas."

"Oh, right. He's totally got it bad for you."

"It doesn't matter. The problem is I'm in way over my head, and I need to back out."

Shay's eyes narrowed with concern. "What the hell happened?"

I quickly summarized the chain of events. It was impossible for the conversation to avoid the vibrator incident. Shay already knew, but she couldn't help mentioning it.

"Oh, my God! I still can't even," she finally said at the tail end of her laughter. "I would've given anything to see Lucas trying to handle that. He tends to be so serious."

While I chose to leave out the fact I'd been a virgin, I did tell her I'd never had a serious relationship. "So I don't know what to do. Things felt pretty intense, and then after the night I babysat, he pretty much shut down. It's like nothing ever happened," I finally said.

Shay was quiet for a few beats before she finally spoke. "Well, I'm not an expert. Let's make that crystal clear. I have more experience with bad relationships than with good. This thing with Jackson is just crazy luck for me."

I couldn't help it, and I cut her off. "We never talked about it, but I know what you went through. My parents actually prayed for you, just so you know."

She put her hand on her chest, her eyes wide. "Are you serious?"

"Oh, yes. They wanted you to be safe. In fact, I went home for a visit after I got the job here, and I told them you were doing well. After all that, it's not easy for you to be okay. So maybe it feels like luck for you to find Jackson, but it's not like it just magically happened."

Shay reached across the table to squeeze my hand. "Thank you." Pausing, she swallowed as she released my hand to take a sip of coffee. "Anyway, back to you. Apparently, Lucas doesn't *ever* get involved. Jackson didn't say much about it, but he did tell me he thinks Lucas really likes you."

"So what if he does? He has a daughter to worry about, and that's his priority, as it should be. I totally understand him having some reservations about getting involved with someone."

"That's something every single parent deals with. I think you should let him know how you feel and see how he responds."

"I don't know how I feel!" I exclaimed.

"Okay, when you imagine things ending now, how does that feel?"

My heart got that same stinging sensation it did whenever I saw Lucas. "Not good," I said with a sigh.

Shay's smile unfurled slowly. "Well, maybe you should think about that. From what I see, you like him. A lot. And I don't think it's just about sex. No matter what, Lucas is a solid guy. Family means everything to him."

Although I didn't think she meant for me to interpret her comment the way I did, it was illuminating in a blinding flash of light. Family *was* everything to him. Which was precisely why he would proceed with extreme caution at even the idea of trying to bring someone into his and Rylie's life.

There was that and the fact that, despite my own intense feelings for him, for all I knew, he felt nothing more than lust for me. I didn't doubt the nearly incendiary attraction between us, but the rest, well, there was no way for me to know.

Because of his priorities, which I completely respected, considering the idea of navigating the risky terrain of a relationship was more than I could ask.

"What? What's that look for?" Shay asked.

I glanced away, looking out the window where the sun was sliding down the sky, its light casting at an angle through the window, the soft gold rays warm in the air-conditioned room. Looking back at Shay, I shrugged and sighed. "That kind of sums it all up, doesn't it?"

Shay leaned forward. "What the hell are you talking about?"

"Family means everything to him. Rylie is his priority, and she should be. I think I need to stop worrying and realize that's just where he's at. Trying to push something when I don't even know what I really want certainly doesn't make sense."

Shay shook her head. "Of course family's important, but that doesn't mean Lucas should never get serious with anyone. That's crazy. I happen to know his sister, and I know from her—"

I cut in. "I met her, and it was pretty clear she was *not* thrilled to meet me."

Shay rolled her eyes. "Okay, whatever. Not having been there, I can't speak to that. Just think about it."

"Think about what?"

"Telling him how you feel," she replied rather emphatically.

"I think first I have to figure out how I feel. Even then, it's best if I don't get my hopes up. I'd rather just be his friend and leave it at that."

I wasn't feeling at all resolved from this conversation. I didn't think Shay was about to let me off the hook, but there was a quick knock on the door, and we both looked over to find Jackson there.

"Mind manning the front?" he asked Shay.

"Of course not," she said, standing quickly. "What's up?"

"An emergency surgery. I'm gonna need help from Skylar, so she won't be at the front."

"On it." Shay stood quickly. Just as she reached the door, she glanced back, her eyes catching mine. "Do you mind feeding the animals?"

"Of course not," I replied quickly. "Consider it done."

"Thanks," she called over her shoulder as she hurried down the hallway.

I got a little bit more done out of sheer stubbornness because not being able to focus annoyed me to no end. I managed to finish a few reports regarding ordering and budgeting before it was time to start the rounds of feeding.

I went to the rescue barn first because going there always made me smile. Gloria was waddling along the fence line between the pastures and kept me company as I crossed over. The horses were still out in one pasture, gathered in a corner under the shade of the big willow beside the pond. The air was heavy today. Even though it was early evening, stepping outside the air conditioning felt like hitting a blast of heat. My skin was instantly damp and sticky from the humidity.

I reached down, scratching behind Gloria's ears. She made her a little snuffling sound and bumped her nose against my knees. Once I got to the rescue barn, I went through the rounds. I'd learned to deal with the goats first because they were bossy and made noise the whole time if I didn't.

Once they were settled, I moved on to deal with the dogs. The dogs rotated more than any of the other rescues. We'd taken in two more last week. One of them, a sweet older hound mix, nudged her head against my thigh when I stepped into her kennel to feed her. I stayed with her a few extra minutes making sure she was comfortable when I heard Squeaky outside.

I fetched a carrot out of my pocket and offered it to her as she came through the door. After taking care of her and Gloria, I headed out to deal with the horses. I realized as I was walking over that I had to take care of the stallion alone. According to Shay, Jackson was looking high and low for another place for him because he wasn't fitting in well. He figured the stallion needed a place with less horses and more space.

The other times I helped with feeding, Lucas had dealt with the stallion. I didn't like thinking about that, so I kicked those thoughts right out of my mind. I started with the other horses first. The stallion was nowhere to be found. After a few calls, I figured my only choice was to go find him.

Through the trees in the corner, I saw a shadow moving, so I walked in that direction, sticking close to the fence. At the sound of hooves pounding, I looked up to see him burst through the trees. Racing straight toward me, he let out a rumbling neigh and threw his head up.

My heart started to beat wildly, and fear had my feet frozen to the ground. At the last minute, I came out of my stupor and dashed toward the fence line, but it was too late. The stallion raced straight at me, dodging at the last minute and kicking his feet up.

Pain struck the back of my head, sharp and jolting.

I heard someone calling my name as I fell. There was a glancing thud against my shoulder and then everything went black.

Chapter Twenty-Nine

LUCAS

I parked over at the clinic to check in with Jackson about the first responder schedule before I went home. When I heard the sound of a horse galloping and glanced over to see Valentina directly in the line of sight with the stallion, my heart stopped.

I broke into a run. "Valentina!"

The horse kicked as he blew past her, clipping the back of her head, and she fell limply to the ground. The horse kept on, circling in front of the paddock and aiming for the far end of the pasture. Panic clogged my throat and sent my pulse lunging.

"Valentina!"

My eyes scanned the ground as I reached the edge of the pasture, distantly aware of someone calling my name. I ignored it. Ducking, I stepped through the lower pole of the fence and dashed to her side.

Her red hair was bright against the ground. Her skin was pale, and her head lolled to the side. Kneeling in the dirt with the air hot and sticky around us, I pressed two fingers to the pulse on her neck, finding it rapid and shallow. I kept telling myself to be calm, but inside, I felt completely disoriented.

My brain fuzzed with panic. Despite my heart thrashing in my chest and fear beating like a drum in my thoughts, I functioned mostly on autopilot. I hadn't been a first responder for almost a decade for nothing. After checking her pulse, I quickly checked to make sure nothing had been broken, then I moved to lift her in my arms.

Only to stop abruptly when I heard my name. Glancing over my shoulder, I saw Dawson jogging over, carrying a lightweight portable stretcher in one hand. "Slow your roll, man," he said as he reached me and stepped through the fence. "She took quite a hit. I saw it from the barn. Wade and I came over to check on some supplies. Ryan's headed out to wrangle the stallion. Let me help you lift her onto the stretcher."

I almost barked at him and told him to get the hell away because I wanted Valentina close to me, but I knew he was being smart, and I wasn't.

Within a minute, he had the lightweight stretcher unfolded on the ground and helped me ease her onto it. I kept wanting her to wake up and open her eyes. But she didn't.

Out of the corner of my eye, I saw Ryan jogging along the fence toward the trees. At this point, I didn't think we were at risk. The stallion might be a fucking asshole, but I knew damn well he hadn't intended to hurt Valentina. He was just full of it.

We walked alongside the fence to the gate. Dawson was quiet and calm, which I appreciated. He was a jokester when it wasn't serious, but all business when it was. He had a remarkably steady presence. I trusted everyone on our crew. By chance, I had worked the most with him and Jackson, and knew Dawson was rock solid.

If he had an opinion about my reaction, it didn't show. Meanwhile, my eyes kept flicking to Valentina. Her head had rolled to the side when we shifted her onto the stretcher. I wanted her to wake up. I needed to know she was okay. When we reached the barn, Wade had the emergency vehicle Jackson kept on site idling in the parking area between the vet clinic and house. Dawson and I shifted Valentina onto the wheeled stretcher and slid it into the back of the van.

"You riding with?" Dawson asked, looking straight at me.

"Of course."

He simply nodded, not even asking if I was riding in the front. I climbed in beside Valentina, pulling the doors shut in the back. My throat was tight, and my heart felt as if it was about to explode. Part of me wanted to argue the point and say we didn't need to take her to the hospital, but I knew better. Head injuries had a protocol, and it sure as hell didn't involve blowing off a full medical evaluation.

Dawson and Wade were up front, and Wade peeled out, gravel spinning behind the tires as he flicked on the emergency lights and sirens. The hospital in Stolen Hearts Valley was no more than ten minutes away, but it was winding mountain roads every mile between the lodge and downtown.

I barely noticed anything, dimly aware of Dawson and Wade's hushed conversation and their occasional calls back to ask me how Valentina was doing.

"Fine," I kept saying. Except she wasn't conscious yet, so I didn't know if I was only saying that to trick myself into believing she was. Maybe if I said it enough, she would be guaranteed to be fine.

Thoughts barreled through my mind, slamming into me. My regret ran deep—at the distance I had put between us recently and wondering just what the hell I was thinking.

Mine, mine, mine repeated on a loop. I'd made a huge fucking mistake. It was a mistake thinking I shouldn't give us a shot. The idea of losing her utterly terrified me. I couldn't stop thinking of that possibility.

You're not gonna fucking lose her.
You don't know. You just can't know that.

Head injuries were weird. People died. I knew that. Just like Melissa, Valentina could be gone.

It felt like forever and no time at all when Wade pulled into the circular drive at the emergency room entrance. They swung into action. At least for this part, my autopilot worked. I helped them get Valentina out, and we jogged in through the ER doors, wheeling her on the stretcher.

I wanted to go with her to the examining room, but it wasn't an option. This was the part where we handed her over to someone else's care. I didn't want to let her go, suddenly concerned that whoever took over wouldn't get it right.

Wade caught my arm. "Come on, man. Let them do their thing."

My feet were rooted to the floor as the medical team shifted into gear, taking the stretcher from us and hurrying down the hallway. I looked into Wade's calm brown gaze and simply nodded, turning with him and walking down the hall in silence.

I sank into a chair in the waiting room, surprised when Wade sat down beside me. Glancing over, I asked, "Don't you need to deal with the van?"

"Nah. Dawson's got it."

"You don't have to wait with me."

I was quite certain I saw something like sympathy flicker in his eyes. "I'm waiting. Dawson'll be back soon, and we'll wait with you."

I was too numb to cry, but the burn in my eyes and my throat was intense.

We waited in silence. I realized the last time I'd been at the hospital was when Melissa died. She collapsed at work, and I got a call from the receptionist where she worked to let me know they'd called 911. By the time I got to the hospital, she'd already been declared dead, but I wouldn't find that out right away. I had to wait for the doctor. Rylie had been with my mother that afternoon. It had been all I could do not to completely fall apart.

As brutal as that event was, somehow this felt worse. I didn't mean to make it sound as though it wasn't horrible that Melissa died. It was. It was just that I hadn't known what I might be facing then. My fear now was smothering, perhaps because I knew what a loss like this could feel like.

Dawson returned. He and Wade were blessedly quiet, not expecting anything from me. Dawson fetched us all coffee and handed me one of those thin paper cups.

After I took a sip and then another, he cleared his throat from where he sat across from me. "All right, man, I'm not one for lots of advice, but I just have one thing to say."

When my eyes swung up to meet his, he nodded firmly. "Stop being a fucking idiot about her. It's pretty obvious."

"What's obvious?" I asked, promptly demonstrating my ability to be said idiot.

Wade sighed heavily. "That you love her."

For just a second, the part of me that had closed ranks after Melissa died wanted to snap back at him. The rest of my heart smacked that voice upside the head. *You do love her.*

I swallowed, chasing the pain knotted in my throat with another sip of semi-cold shitty coffee, and nodded. "I know."

"Thank fuck for small favors," Wade said, leaning his head against the wall.

"Maybe you'll be in a better mood now," Dawson added with a chuckle, finally letting out a bit of his teasing side.

After a moment, a woman in a white coat came out, glancing around. "Family for Valentina Smith?"

I jumped up, crossing the room swiftly, realizing just then I should probably call her parents. I didn't even know them, much less how to reach them. I needed to remedy that soon.

"Right here," I said as I stopped in front of her. I was willing to lie if necessary. "I'm her boyfriend."

The doctor paused and then carried on. "Ms. Smith

should be fine. She's awake now. Given the tests we ran, she should be cleared for release in another hour. She'll need someone with her for the next twenty-four hours to wake her every two hours."

"She'll be with me," I replied swiftly. "Can I see her?"

When I stepped into Valentina's room minutes later, her eyes widened when she saw me. My heart finally relaxed, but my emotions were still spinning wildly through me, making me feel half crazy.

Approaching the bed carefully, I stopped at her side, looking down. Her red hair was bright against the white pillows propped up behind her. Although she wasn't as pale as she'd been earlier, her freckles stood out against her skin.

"You gave me a scare," I said, reaching to curl my hand around hers where it rested by her side. Her skin was cool, and I wanted to make her warm.

"I gave myself a scare. That stallion's an asshole."

The mere mention of the stallion flying by and kicking her brought my fear rushing back and set my heart to pounding.

Valentina's eyes coasted over my face, her brow furrowing. "Are you okay? And what are you doing here?"

Her hand curled into mine, squeezing slightly with her questions. Of course she would be worried about me. "I'm okay but only because you're okay," I said, my voice coming out scratchy. "I'm here because I was near the pasture and saw the stallion knock you out with a kick."

I tried to gather my thoughts, to say something sensible, but nothing felt sensible now. "I screwed up. I'm sorry. I thought, well, I thought it wasn't a good idea to let Rylie get ideas. I guess I thought I should wait, but I can't. You're too important." I dived into the deep end of this conversation so fast, I startled myself. But I couldn't put this off.

Valentina's eyes widened just as a nurse came in, all business.

"Okay, dear, we need to do a few checks. You're gonna have to sit tight for at least an hour."

"But I feel fine," Valentina insisted.

Looking into her eyes, I sensed she did not enjoy feeling at the mercy of the hospital. "You're going to wait until they say it's okay for you to leave. Then you're coming home with me."

All the while, my heart kept up that steady, almost thrashing beat. She seemed okay, but I wasn't going to relax until we got through tomorrow.

Chapter Thirty

VALENTINA

I felt everything—every inch of my body. My head carried a dull ache, and subtle pains throbbed in random places. I presumed my fall had jolted me enough everywhere and figured I'd find a few bruises later.

All the while, even though I was a little confused with Lucas's shift, I was so relieved he was here. He rarely left the room while I was waiting. Others stopped by to see me. I learned Dawson had delivered Lucas's truck to him so he could drive me home and was catching a ride back to the lodge with Wade.

Dani visited for a little bit. She and Lucas had a tense conversation in the corner of the room. It ended with her words carrying across the room to me. *"You better not screw this up."*

She'd spun away from him and cast me a smile. She braided my hair for me even though I told her it wasn't necessary. Just before she left, she leaned over and whispered in my ear, "I think Lucas is in love with you, so you might want to figure out how you feel."

I had so many questions, but I was tired, and all of my

questions were emotional landmines. I felt as if my emotions were pressing against my skin, almost bursting through. With the state of my headache, I didn't think I was in the best place to try to have an emotional conversation with Lucas.

When we arrived at his house, I was surprised to discover Rylie wasn't there. When I glanced his way in the truck, he answered my unspoken question. "She's at my parents' for the night. I texted them while we were waiting at the hospital."

Without further comment, Lucas rounded the truck and lifted me into his arms to carry me inside. Although I found having so many people hovering at the hospital disconcerting, I discovered I liked being held in his arms. I liked it a lot. He set me down on the couch, still quiet. He gave off an intensity I didn't quite know how to interpret.

Glancing down, he said, "Your call. We can sleep out here or in my bedroom, but I'm supposed to wake you every two hours."

Selfishly, I wanted the comfort of his bed. That way, he would be right beside me. I might not have had many nights with Lucas, but I loved every single one.

"Bedroom."

He graced me with the first smile I'd seen from him in weeks. "You got it, darlin'."

Turning away, he crossed the room to kick his shoes off by the door before walking down the hallway. I started to get up and follow him, but he was back in a flash.

"All I was doing was straightening the covers. I'm not the best about making my bed every day."

"I can walk, you know," I protested as he approached.

"I don't care," he replied, swinging me into his arms again.

As much as I wanted to insist, the feel of being held in his strong embrace was too tempting. It was late, going on eleven at night.

"Have you eaten?" I asked. I'd had a not so good hospital meal, but I wasn't particularly hungry.

"Sure did. While I waited at the hospital, I snacked. I'm just fine."

He carried me into his bedroom and eased me down onto the bed. "Since I didn't have a chance to get you any clothes, you can sleep in one of my T-shirts," he explained gruffly, gesturing to a clean white shirt folded on the pillow beside me.

I didn't quite know what to make of any of this. Too weary to be tidy, I let my leggings and shirt fall in a pile on the floor. I changed into his T-shirt, leaving on my underwear, and undid the braid in my hair while he stepped into the bathroom. It smelled like him, crisp and clean. They'd let me shower at the hospital, so I was ready for bed.

Lucas returned from the bathroom wearing nothing but a pair of black fitted boxer briefs. I suddenly realized that while I might not be up for an emotional conversation, my body could still have a reaction to his delectable bare chest. Damn. My belly tightened.

He set his smartphone on the nightstand and slipped under the covers. The sheets were cool, and I found myself wanting to burrow against him. While it was hot outside, I'd been in an air-conditioned hospital for hours now.

"I'm setting my alarm to go off every two hours. Here's the deal," he began, his eyes canting down to mine. "If you don't wake up, we are going straight to the hospital, and I'm calling them on the way."

"They said I was fine. My head hurts a little, but that's it." I lifted my hand, gently touching the tender area on the side of my head behind my ear.

"I know. You're going to be fine," he said, his words firm.

I was too tired to think about it and cuddled against his side, the tension unraveling slowly inside. His shoulders shifted slightly as he reached over and turned off the lamp beside the bed.

"Lucas?" I asked into the dark room a few moments later.

"Mm-hmm?" he murmured as his fingers sifted through my hair.

"How come you brought me here tonight?"

"Let's talk about that tomorrow morning."

That was the last thing I remembered before I fell asleep.

Chapter Thirty-One

LUCAS

That night with Valentina was a strange type of hell. I barely slept. I had my alarm set, but it was entirely unnecessary. As the doctor ordered, I woke Valentina every other hour. She reliably woke up, and I felt like I could finally relax as dawn approached.

One thing crystallized in my mind during the night—how I felt about her. I didn't quite know how it happened, but I suspected it was because I truly hadn't expected it. Valentina had slipped into my heart, curling around it effortlessly and pulling me straight into love. Perhaps because it was so easy to be with her.

She was so open and so honest, a rare combination of innocent and wise. While I'd thought no one could ever be in my heart again, Valentina shredded that belief with nothing more than a look.

After that night of waiting, I knew my own feelings with certainty. Yet I didn't know if she felt anything close to the way I did.

The most terrifying part of it all was realizing I had to

make myself vulnerable. There were plenty of reasons for Valentina to be wary because I had shut her out.

When I woke her at the last prescribed time, and her blue eyes blinked open, I breathed a sigh of relief. Sagging against the pillows propped against the headboard, I curled my arm around her shoulders, holding her close to my side. "Thank fucking God," I muttered.

"I'm pretty sure you're going to break me of worrying about swearing," she said with a soft laugh.

I chuckled. "I did notice every so often you slap your hand over your mouth when you swear."

She sighed. "Habit from growing up with my parents. It's fine. Oh my God, I should call them," she said, sitting up suddenly.

I handed her my phone. "I don't know where the hell your phone is. You can call them with mine. I would've called them last night for you, but I didn't have their number."

"I need to shower first. And maybe have some coffee."

"Works for me," I replied.

She shifted, kicking the covers away and swinging her feet off the bed. I was tempted to carry her to the bathroom. As if she read my mind, she said, "I don't even have a headache. It's just a little sore where he kicked me. I'm walking to the shower."

I sighed and nodded, relieved to see her spunk back in full force. I followed her into the bathroom off the side of my bedroom.

If she had any hesitation about changing in front of me, she didn't show it, stripping down and climbing in as the water began to steam. I didn't ask if I could join her and quickly slid my briefs off before stepping into the shower behind her.

Valentina looked my way, her eyes flicking down to my arousal. Because, yeah, I couldn't be around her naked and not get aroused. When her eyes swung to mine, she was smiling.

"Ignore it."

"What if I don't want to?" she parried, her eyes darkening.

"Valentina," I warned.

She put a palm on my chest, pressing me against the tile wall. With steam cloaking us, water rolling over her curves, and her tight nipples pressing against me, I didn't know if I had the willpower to stop her.

"Darlin', I want to get this right, and a quickie in the shower wasn't what I had in mind," I managed to choke out.

"A quickie in the shower is exactly right. I've never had one."

After that, I was a goner. When she leaned up to kiss me, I dived into the warm sweetness of her mouth as my hands slid over her slick wet curves.

Moments later when I was buried inside her with her back against the tile and her legs wrapped around my waist, her tight pussy nearly sent me over the edge instantly. I held still, feeling the silky clench of her channel rippling around me.

"Look at me," I murmured.

Her eyes fluttered open, the blue bright against her freckled cheeks. "What?"

"I love you." Saying a mere three words had my heart pounding so hard it almost hurt.

She held my gaze quietly. She lifted her hand, her finger tracing around my mouth. "That's a good thing," she said softly, "because I love you too. I might not be an expert, but I do know what love is."

My forehead fell to hers as I tried to breathe through the emotion racing through me. "I didn't expect you to tell me the same. Are you ...?"

Valentina shook her head slightly. "You know me. I say whatever's on my mind, and I *definitely* mean it."

Swallowing, I lifted my head slightly to press a quick kiss to her lips. I had no more words.

"Sometimes I say too much," she added.

I laughed a little, recalling that fateful afternoon on her porch when I heard all about why she ordered a pink vibrator.

No more words were necessary. The water sluiced over us. I held her tight and rocked into her until I felt her tighten, and she cried my name. Only then did I let go, my release slamming through me so hard it was a good thing I had my hand on the wall to hold me up.

After that, we used the shower for its original intention. We dressed, and she made me breakfast. I discovered she could make amazing waffles. Rylie was due home soon, and I was toying with what I was going to say. I looked over at her, and asked, "How do you want us to handle this with Rylie?"

Valentina was refilling our coffees and turned back, two mugs held in her hands. Her gaze was sober, and she was quiet as she returned to the table. "Slowly. One step at a time."

Much as I wanted to rush, her answer was exactly what I needed to hear. I would've rushed, but that was why my heart knew Valentina was perfect.

EPILOGUE

Valentina

A year or so later

I was folding laundry. If I was ever bored, laundry was forever there for me. Lots of it. Between Rylie and Lucas, it was endless. I closed Rylie's dresser and carried the laundry basket into the bedroom I shared with Lucas. A hint of bright pink winked at me when I opened our shared under-wear drawer.

That vibrator was a favorite one for us. Grinning, I put away Lucas's boxers and my panties. Just as I closed the drawer to our dresser, I heard the front door open and close. Puzzled, I walked down the hallway, only to stop in my tracks when I saw Lucas.

"What are you doing here?" I asked, my heart stumbling and tripping a little.

It didn't matter I'd only seen him a few hours earlier because every damn time I saw him my pulse took off and butterflies twirled in my belly.

His gaze swept over me, making my skin prickle all over.

"The group I was supposed to take on a hike today cancelled. I thought I'd come home for lunch."

Somehow, I sensed his idea of lunch had nothing to do with food. Cocking my head to the side, I asked, "And what do you want for lunch?"

His lashes brushed against his cheeks as he closed his eyes. When he opened them again slowly, the look contained there stole my breath. "You."

There went the rest of my day. Or at least the next hour.

Sometime later, Lucas was propped up against the headboard while I trailed my fingertips over his chest, marveling at the hard, muscled planes. My eyes flicked to the clock across the nightstand behind his shoulder. "We have to get dressed," I murmured.

"Do we now?" he asked in reply. He caught one of my curls between two fingers and pulled it out, letting it bounce against my cheek.

"Rylie gets off the bus in a half hour."

I lifted my head. His teasing expression was suddenly gone. He'd already left me boneless and sated, but the intensity in his eyes now set my heart pounding all over again. "What?"

The sound of his swallow was audible in the quiet. His chest pressed against my breasts when he took a deep breath, and his hand tightened slightly in my hair and loosened before he spoke. "I've been thinking." There was a long pause, and I started to get nervous. "Things with us feel good, really good. I keep telling myself nothing is perfect, nothing is forever, but I don't care. I meant to make it an event, but now just seems like the time. Because I can't imagine life without you."

Blood rushed through my ears at the ragged, hopeful beat of my heart. I could hardly catch my breath. Emotion clenched in my chest, tightening in my throat. "What do you mean?"

"I mean I want you to marry me." His words came out husky, a hint of uncertainty contained in them.

"Are you sure?"

Lucas was a man who held his emotions so close that it was hard to imagine he had tears in his eyes. But I was pretty sure that was what I saw. "Of course I'm sure."

I rose, straddling his hips. "Yes! One hundred percent yes."

"Oh, thank God," he murmured as he pulled me close, his forehead leaning against mine. "For a second there, I thought you were gonna tell me no."

I pressed my lips to his, pulling away just far enough to speak. "There was never any doubt." Pausing, I dragged my fingertip along his stubbled jawline. "My parents will be thrilled, you know. They try not to badger me, but I know we're probably the source of extra prayers since we've been living in sin."

Lucas chuckled. "Your father has mentioned it more than once, but that's not why I'm asking."

"I know, but you do have Rylie and plenty of reasons for waiting."

"I want you. This. Us," he said firmly. "The next part is telling Rylie. She's been asking me for a while."

I was stunned. I loved Rylie. She was getting to be a bit of a handful because she was a spirited girl. I felt so blessed to be able to share this time with her, yet I had tried so, *so* hard not to make any presumptions about what Lucas and I had.

"Really?"

He nodded, one of his slow smiles unfurling and making my belly clench. "Of course. You're her mother in every way that counts. Melissa will always be the mother she had first, but Rylie doesn't remember her." Lifting a hand, he slid his fingers through my curls, the heat and love in his eyes almost undoing me. Seeing as we were still naked in bed, my body had its own thoughts as I felt his cock swell slightly under me.

"We have to get dressed," I said firmly, scrambling off his lap.

His low chuckle followed me into the shower where we might have wasted a little more time.

————

LUCAS

Another six months later

Opening the front door, my eyes veered toward the kitchen. Valentina's dark red curls were up in a messy ponytail, and Rylie's hair was falling loose from its braid.

Valentina stood at the kitchen counter, chopping vegetables. Rylie was standing on a wide stepstool beside her, one I had built for her to be able to help in the kitchen. Valentina was getting dinner ready while Rylie was working beside her on the cookies for dessert.

My heart clenched. I loved coming home to them every night.

They appeared to hear me at the same time. Valentina set her knife down and glanced over her shoulder, calling, "Hey, you're home a little early."

She stepped to the sink to rinse her hands. Meanwhile, Rylie clambered down, not bothering to wash her hands, and ran across the room to fling her arms around my waist. She added a few handprints of flour to my dusty jeans.

"Hey there," I murmured as I pressed a kiss to the top of her head.

"Hey, Daddy," she said, spinning immediately around and hurrying back to her cookies.

Valentina approached as I let my bag fall to the floor.

Stopping in front of me, she lifted her hand, brushing her thumb across my cheek. "You have dirt on your face," she observed with a slight smile.

"And you have flour on yours," I countered, brushing my knuckles across the powdery white streak along her jaw.

I pulled her close, dusting kisses at the corners of her mouth. "Remind me I get to come home to this every night," I murmured softly.

"Consider yourself reminded. Always."

Having loved and lost once, "always" had a different connotation for me. But I would take every single second I had with Valentina.

———

Thank you for reading Wait For Me - I hope you loved Lucas & Valentina's story!

Up next in the Swoon Series is Break My Fall - Dawson & Evie's story. Dawson is a player, and Evie has no intention of falling for him. *Absolutely* not.

Dawson thinks he's immune to love. Just won't happen. Yet, Evie brings him to his knees. It's a scorching hot friends to lovers romance. Don't miss their story!

Keep reading for a sneak peek!

Be sure to sign up for my newsletter for the latest news, teasers & more! Click here to sign up: http://jhcroixauthor.com/subscribe/

EXCERPT: BREAK MY FALL

Dawson

A waiter weaved through the crowd, a tray of wines and beers in hand. He paused beside me, and I snagged a pint of beer. The hum of conversation carried on around me. Usually, I was in my element like this. I could dive in, drink a little too much, party a little too hard, and flirt like there was no tomorrow. Preferably, a night like this would end with a warm and willing woman in my bed.

Lately, I was clinging to the concept of "fake it until you make it."

An unmistakable voice drew my attention. "Oh my God!" Evie Blair exclaimed.

Following the sound, I saw Evie nudge some guy in the shoulder as he smiled down at her. By the angle of his eyes, I surmised he was catching a healthy glimpse of her cleavage. An entirely irrational streak of possessiveness jolted me. I didn't get possessive, much less jealous.

Shaking the feeling off, I took the moment to absorb her. Evie was lovely, although not in any typical way. Oh, she had glossy hair dark that fell straight down her back and stunning rich, blue eyes. I couldn't look into them for too long, it felt as if I were diving, straight into the deep sea. I never knew if I'd be able to come up for air. With her slightly crooked nose, lopsided smile, and a dusting of freckles across the bridge of her nose, she was downright endearing. She was short with hips that swung with every step.

I dragged my eyes away from her, lifting my beer to my lips. I lowered it a second later and turned to set it on a counter along the wall behind me. I had no interest in drinking. All of my usual tricks were failing me.

"Hey man," a voice said over my shoulder.

Glancing to the side, I found Wade Ellis standing there. "Hey," I replied, forcing some semblance of a smile on my face.

"Not even drinking tonight," he commented.

Shaking my head, I shrugged. "Nah. I'm here to support the lodge, but that's about it."

Lost Deer Winery, a premier winery in the Blue Ridge Mountains, was hosting a fundraiser for Stolen Hearts Rescue, an animal rescue program on the run by the same place I worked.

I wasn't up for conversation and, blessedly, someone else said something to Wade, and he turned away to reply. Glancing at my watch, I calculated I'd been here for a solid hour, more than enough time. If necessary, I would claim I had headache. In a way, I did.

Turning, I clapped Wade's shoulder as I passed by and started to thread through the crowd. I wasn't paying much attention to where I was going when Evie's voice caught my ears, dragging my gaze sideways to where she stood only a few feet away.

"Excuse me?" Her tone was sharp.

Without thinking, I veered closer, stopping at her side just as the man who had been staring down her cleavage curled his hand around her upper arm. Her skin dimpled under his grip, deep enough I figured he'd leave bruises. I cut between them, shouldering the asshole out of the way.

The man's dark gaze swung to me, his mouth opening as if to protest. I glared at him, and he snapped his mouth shut. "What the fuck, dude?" he muttered as he released Evie's arm.

My eyes flicked down, noticing the red splotches left from his fingerprints on the soft curve of her bicep. "You okay?" I asked, glancing to Evie.

She looked up, a pink tinge cresting on her cheeks. "I'm fine." She looked back to the man. "Back the fuck off, asshole."

The guy simply snorted and shook his head before turning away. Another waiter walked past us just as a woman turned quickly, her shoulder colliding with the tray and sending three glasses of wine tipping to the side, red wine splashing all over Evie's dress.

"Gah!" Evie exclaimed, jumping back.

Evie didn't wear dresses too often. In fact, I didn't know if I'd ever seen her in one. The dress in question was a light, shimmery cream fabric. With a fitted bodice, it fell to her knees in a twirl, the sweet curve of her hips tempting me to run my hands over them. I didn't think it was meant to show off her curves, but with her, it was impossible for them not to show. She'd paired her dress with a pair of chunky black boots, which suited her perfectly.

Her dress was now stained red all over the front. Evie looked down and sighed, eyeing the wine stains running in streaks. With the waiter murmuring his apologies and the woman who'd run into the tray chiming in, Evie simply shrugged. "It happens. Leave it to me to take the wine tasting far more seriously than anyone else," she added with a laugh.

A genuine smile stretched across my face for what felt like the first time in weeks. Evie had that effect on me. There was something so real about her it was hard not to smile.

The waiter interjected, "Ma'am, can I bring you a towel or anything?"

She shrugged. "Not much point to it. I guess I'll cut out early." Her eyes scanned the room.

"Want a ride?" I asked.

I knew by chance she'd caught a ride here with Dani. Like me, Evie lived at Stolen Hearts Lodge where we both worked.

"You're leaving?" she countered, sounding surprised.

For good reason. I wasn't usually wont to leave anything resembling a party early. I just couldn't find the mood for them the last few weeks.

I met her gaze and nodded. "I was on my way out when I passed by."

"Okay." She glanced down at her wine stained dress. "My dress is ruined."

I shrugged. "Maybe. Come on," I said, gesturing toward the exit at the back.

Evie fell into step beside me before stopping. "Wait a second, I need to let the girls know I'm leaving." She spun away, threading through the crowd and ignoring the glances at her wine stained dress. She stopped beside Shay and Dani, pointing at her dress and shaking her head. Shay's eyes met mine across the room, and I could sense her curiosity. I didn't usually leave early for anything.

Within a moment, Evie returned my side. "Okay. Take me home."

Reflexively, I slipped my arm around her shoulders as we walked through the crowded winery. As soon as my hand landed on the curve of her shoulder, I became acutely aware of her silky skin. Her scent drifted to me, a hint of sugar and cream. I wanted to bury my nose in her hair. My hyper awareness of her didn't make any sense. Or perhaps it did.

"Shay and Jackson are gonna make gobs of money for the rescue," Evie said just as we reached the door.

"I'll say, and that's a good thing. Jackson was commenting

last week he's thinking of expanding the rescue program."

Her eyes canted up to mine as I held the door for her. "Really?" Answering her own question, she continued, "Well, it's full all the time anyway."

The door swung shut behind us as we stepped outside into the soft autumn air.

Fall in the Blue Ridge Mountains was definitely cooler than summer, a relief from the heat that hung over the land-scape like a heavy curtain on the hottest days.

Our footsteps crunched as we walked across the gravel parking lot. I took a breath, feeling a subtle sense of ease inside. I hadn't felt like myself for going on a month. Just now though, I felt a little lighter.

Evie didn't ask where my truck was and seemed content to follow me. I looked ahead. Lost Deer Winery sat on the hillside with a view out over Stolen Hearts Valley. The famous blue haze of the Blue Ridge Mountains was fading into the darkness, a mist shimmering above the mountain ridge in the distance.

The moon's silvery light cast everything in an ethereal glow. I took a deep breath, inhaling the air earth scented with fallen leaves.

"Where...?"

Evie's question trailed off when I slid my hand down her back, angling her with a gentle, coaxing pressure on her low back to where my truck was.

"Oh, there it is," she said brightly.

Out of habit, I went to the passenger side and opened the door for her. Evie looked up at me, and I wanted to kiss her. With the moonlight on her hair, her eyes were a silvery blue, wide with surprise. "Well geez, Dawson, I didn't know you could be a gentleman."

My laugh surprised me. Evie was easy to be with—so, so easy. That was a gift.

"Amazing, isn't it?" I countered.

A smile teasing her lips, she climbed in, tucking her skirt

carefully around her legs. With her smile buoying me, I closed the door and rounded the front of my truck, my body humming with anticipation. Evie's presence was a scattering of sparks on the fire banked between us. It had been there since I first met her.

Always.

I usually ignored it and deflected it with humor—because its potency frightened me a bit. With her haphazard beauty, her quirky personality, and her underlying sassy sweetness, she struck me as a woman who might not be satisfied with casual. As much as I wanted her, I hewed to what was safe so far.

During the drive, I felt her gaze on me and slid mine sideways when I came to a stop sign. In the dark cab of my truck, the air suddenly felt charged.

If only because Evie's presence had nudged me out of the edge of darkness where I'd been mentally teetering for weeks, I managed to tease. "Enjoying the view, are you?"

Her mouth dropped open. "Oh my God. You are *so* cocky," she said dryly. Her eyes were flashing, and I knew she enjoyed our banter as much as I did.

Looking away, I chuckled as I pressed my foot pedal to the gas and rolled forward. "I'm only cocky when it's obvious."

"What's obvious?"

"That you were enjoying the view. I wasn't gonna say anything about what the view might be. I don't have an opinion on that."

She burst out laughing, punching my shoulder lightly with her fist. "Let me guess. You rely on the women who throw themselves at your feet for an assessment of your looks."

Sliding my gaze sideways again briefly, I winked before looking back to the road. "Oh no, I rely on the look in your eyes, sugar."

"Jesus, you are *too* much," she murmured. "How much

longer is this drive?"

"Not much." I turned onto the road that led to Stolen Hearts Lodge.

"Thank God. Seriously though, what gives?"

"What do you mean?"

"You, leaving a party without a woman on your arm," she explained.

It was brief, but the sense of coldness that gusted through me was impossible to ignore. I shrugged, striving to keep my tone casual. "Nothing. Just tired. I am human after all."

"Oh, and here I thought you were a vampire," she replied, her tone droll.

My laugh rumbled in my chest. Rolling to a stop, I parked in the area set aside for staff out behind the two renovated barns that comprised the guest portion of the high-end adventure lodge where we worked. The parking lot was tucked in the trees, and several paths branched away from it, leading to guest cabins and staff cabins.

Evie was climbing out by the time I made it around the truck. I reached her just in time to catch her from stumbling. I had parked on the edge of the lot, and her boot slipped on the running board. My arm slipped around her waist as I commented, "Easy there."

A gasp slipped from her lips when she collided against me. Every soft inch of her. Despite working together for two years now, I had never been this close to Evie.

Her eyes swung up to mine. There was nothing but the hazy light of the moon to illuminate the deep blue of her gaze. My breath caught in my throat, and every cell in my body tightened. She was pressed to me. I could feel the tight points of her nipples through her dress.

I wasn't sure if she expected me to move away, but I couldn't seem to make myself do so. My eyes flicked down, snagging on her plush lips. The urge to kiss her was almost overwhelming.

Apparently, it *was* overwhelming. Before I was aware of what I was doing, I was dipping my head and brushing my lips across hers. They were soft and warm, and a little zing of electricity passed between us.

By the time my mind caught up to what was happening, I expected Evie to haul off and slap me. She didn't. Instead, she let out a soft sigh and arched into me.

Just as I was about to fit my mouth over hers and dive in, I checked myself. With another brush of my lips over hers, I forced myself to lift my head. I couldn't force myself to step back just yet though. She felt too good. I was aroused as hell. I was certain she could feel my cock nestled at the apex of her thighs. Because somehow we'd ended up plastered together when all I'd intended to do was help her out of the truck.

My heart was thrashing wildly in my chest, and I was stunned at the way I felt. I felt more alive than I had in months, perhaps in years. And I didn't know what to do with any of it.

When I looked down, her eyes were closed, her dark lashes curled against her cheeks. I desperately wanted to I know what she was thinking, and I just as desperately wanted to extricate myself from this situation.

Not because I wanted to be away from Evie. To the contrary I wanted to carry her through the woods to my cabin. The feeling was foreign to me. I enjoyed women, but my enjoyment was compartmentalized. It was nothing like this humming, driving need to claim her.

Her lashes swept up, her deep blue eyes locking with mine. My heart spun and stopped as if a compass found its magnetic north.

EVIE

Dawson Marsh was warm, tall, and strong. My pulse was

skittering out of control, and I could barely pull my thoughts together.

I was also annoyed as hell with myself. For two long years, even though I thought Dawson was oh-so-tempting, I promised myself I would *not* fall for his charms. He was a master flirt and tease. I didn't need that.

By some miracle, I managed to string together a few words. "What was that?"

When I looked up at Dawson, I expected to see his sly smirk. Instead, he looked as stunned as I felt.

"Hell if I know," he finally said, a wondering laugh slipping free.

That laugh pissed me right the hell off. Just what I needed.

I shimmied out from between the truck and where he stood, stalking away. "Thanks for the ride home," I called over my shoulder.

The sound of his truck door closing carried to me with his footsteps jogging across the gravel next. "Evie!" he called.

———

Coming October 2019!
Break My Fall

If you love steamy, small town romance, take a visit to Willow Brook, Alaska in my Into The Fire Series. Check out Burn For Me - a second chance romance for the ages. It's FREE on all retailers! Don't miss Cade & Amelia's story!

Go here to sign up for information on new releases: http://jhcroixauthor.com/subscribe/

FIND MY BOOKS

Thank you for reading Wait For Me! I hope you enjoyed the story. If so, you can help other readers find my books in a variety of ways.

1) Write a review!
2) Sign up for my newsletter, so you can receive information about upcoming new releases & receive a FREE copy of one of my books: http://jhcroixauthor.com/subscribe/
3) Like and follow my Amazon Author page at https://amazon.com/author/jhcroix
4) Follow me on Bookbub at https://www.bookbub.com/authors/j-h-croix
5) Follow me on Instagram at https://www.instagram.com/jhcroix/
6) Like my Facebook page at https://www.facebook.com/jhcroix

Swoon Series
This Crazy Love
Wait For Me
Break My Fall - coming October 2019!
Into The Fire Series
Burn For Me
Slow Burn
Burn So Bad
Hot Mess
Burn So Good
Sweet Fire
Play With Fire
Melt With You
Burn For You
Crash & Burn
Brit Boys Sports Romance
The Play
Big Win
Out Of Bounds
Play Me
Naughty Wish
Diamond Creek Alaska Novels
When Love Comes
Follow Love
Love Unbroken
Love Untamed
Tumble Into Love
Christmas Nights
Last Frontier Lodge Novels
Take Me Home
Love at Last
Just This Once
Falling Fast
Stay With Me
When We Fall
Hold Me Close

<u>Crazy For You</u>
<u>Just Us</u>
Catamount Lion Shifters
<u>Protected Mate</u>
<u>Chosen Mate</u>
<u>Fated Mate</u>
<u>Destined Mate</u>
<u>A Catamount Christmas</u>
Ghost Cat Shifters
<u>The Lion Within</u>
<u>Lion Lost & Found</u>

ACKNOWLEDGMENTS

Hugs & more hugs to my readers! Y'all keep me writing even when I have doubts.

Much gratitude to my author friends for supporting me, cheering on my books, and reminding me I'm not the only crazy one out there. xoxo

Many thanks to my editor for kindly pointing out ways to give Lucas & Valentina the story they deserved, and to Terri D. for so graciously proofreading.

To my detail queens: Janine, Beth P., Terri E., Heather H., & Carolyne B. Thanks for making sure I dust every corner of my stories.

To my family who cheers me on even though I'm certain I'm the oddest of the bunch. The best kind of love is acceptance.

DBC—my heart, my home, and my best friend.

Of course, my dogs because they run with me every morning while I plot in my head and cuddle with me when I need it.

xoxo

J.H. Croix